Equilibrium

Evan Sasman

Title No.: 4307873
ISBN-13: 978-1492300090

Dedicated to the memory of Buster, who didn't wait for change, but impatiently made change happen.

PREFACE

The 1990s had barely begun. There was a protest on the Bad River Reservation at the old Tribal Administration building. I went to interview the protestors and then get a response from the tribal chairman for a story I would write for the newspaper in nearby Ashland, WI.

It was a small protest, by recent standards in and near the Reservation. A handful of men from the tribe stood outside the Administration Building, signs in opposition to casino expansion leaning against an empty oil drum barrel where firewood burned and the protestors stood warming their hands. They picked up their signs when I arrived, waving them so I could get a picture. Gambling, they believed, was bad for the tribe. I took notes, shot the picture and went inside to talk to the tribal chairman.

The chairman was in a temporary office upstairs. The building's basement was flooded and the first floor still showed water damage. The Bad River had spilled its banks. The River spilled its banks regularly. The Tribe was already dealing with it. Construction had begun on a new tribal administration building on higher ground.

Flooding wasn't the biggest concern. Contamination was. The floodwaters could open former industrial landfills near the river.

Industries had abused the reservation that way in the past, used it like they owned it. Logging companies, without consulting the tribe, had clear-cut square miles of land. I had heard more than one account of tankers filled with chemicals driving down back roads at night, pulling up to the Bad River or Lake Superior and opening the spigot. No one was sure what poured out but it couldn't have been good if they were voiding their contents at night.

I found the chairman in his office above the high water mark and sat down to interview him. We talked about the casino expansion. Then we chatted … small talk. He said he could see I was uneasy about something. I told him it was the first anniversary date of my late wife's death. She had died, at age 30, from cancer. She was Cherokee, I said, although I admitted she was probably more Air Force brat than anything.

He stopped the conversation, looked directly at me, then said, "Here's what you have to do."

He told me I needed to go into the woods to a place sacred to me. I might already know such a place, he said. It came to my mind immediately – St. Peter's Dome, where I had scattered my late wife's ashes atop a peak in the Penokee Range.

He then said I needed to sit down there and wait. In time, an animal would come to me. It would carry a message. I would know what that message was by the type of animal and by its behavior.

I did what he had told me. After I had waited about a half hour on the top of the Dome, I saw two eagles flying high above me. They were circling, riding the currents. Suddenly, one eagle broke away and dived toward the forest that, from up there, was 100 feet below where I sat. The other eagle continued to circle in the heavens. The eagle that dove, never returned to that lofty place to rejoin its companion.

I am a writer. In my writing, or in my reading, the works I enjoyed most were those filled with meaningful symbols. To me, this message on that day was both simple and direct. My wife had died. She would stay in the heavens. I needed to let her go and plunge back into life.

That was the first gift given to me by a Bad River tribal member. There would be many more.

That wasn't my first association with Native Americans and tribal communities. There have been associations all my life.

As a child, living near Black River Falls, the seat of the Ho-Chunk Tribe, there had been Native American foster children in our home. My father, a minister, had also worked for the Wisconsin welfare department and the state had sought him out as a potential foster parent. My parents were open-minded, up to a point. They recognized Native Americans as being as human as anyone, but they didn't miss out on opportunities to convert the foster kids.

In my 20s I met a retired librarian from Black River Falls, WI who had made a point of getting to know tribal members when they came to the library. She had invited them to her house across the street for cake, coffee and conversation. They told her bits and pieces of information about tribal life, language and customs. At each visit Frances Perry would write the information on note cards and file them away. By the time she passed away, she had roughly 10,000 such cards. She gave the cards to the Wisconsin Historical Society.

Frances and I spent hours at her little house across from the library talking, sharing cake and coffee. I was having a difficult time in life as is true for most 20-somethings, and I appreciated someone who listened and heard me from a different perspective than was typical in my world.

Even when I moved to Kenosha to find a job, I returned to visit her on occasions. I remember one such visit clearly. I told her a story about a dream I'd had one night. I was walking the streets of the little town where I had grown up, a place called Alma Center. In my dream, it was a cold night and I was wearing my grandfather's old overcoat. I loved that overcoat. It smelled like my grandfather's pipe tobacco. While walking, I reached the sidewalk in front of the my childhood house. I looked up to the second-floor window where my old bedroom was located.

Then, I was surprised to see a hand move the curtain aside and my mother looking down at me. She waved. I thought, that couldn't be. My parents slept in the next bedroom over.

A few days after the dream, I got a letter from my mother. She wrote that the same night as my dream, she wasn't able to sleep. She sat up in bed and, perhaps on a whim, perhaps intuitively, she pushed the curtain aside and saw me standing on the sidewalk in front of the house. I was wearing my grandfather's old overcoat, she wrote. She waved, but I didn't wave back. I looked pre-occupied. And, by the way, she and my father had moved into my old bedroom. It was bigger and had more light.

When I told this story to Frances, she didn't call me crazy. She didn't suggest therapy. She told me a story in return.

The Ho-Chunk, she said, had a long tradition of people who could leave their bodies and travel at night. They were called bear walkers, although they didn't always occupy the bodies of bears. Any animal would do. Here's the accompanying story she told me.

Frances knew an older woman in the tribe, a woman famous for her cooking. Her husband had recently died. Although she missed him, the elderly woman enjoyed being on her own and free from taking care of other people.

There was also an old man in the tribe whose wife had recently died and he had taken a liking to the woman. He made a point of talking to her at tribal gatherings, sampling and then complimenting whatever dish she had brought. She knew he was interested in her but she didn't want to remarry. She tried to rebuff him, but he wasn't getting the message. Still, that wasn't the worst part, the woman told Frances.

At night, he was inhabiting the body of an owl and sitting in a tree branch outside her bedroom window, hooting at her and keeping her awake all night. It was getting annoying, she said, and she wasn't sleeping well. She planned to see a spiritual woman to get a necklace and some medicine that would keep him away.

Once again, a Native American story arrived when I needed it.

When my daughter was born, we named her after her Cherokee grandmother. But after my wife died, I didn't feel I knew enough about Native American culture to teach her about that side of her heritage. Through a strange twist of events, I was hired to teach English at the Bad River Tribal School. But while I was teaching, I was also learning things I would need to teach my daughter.

Fate had delivered me where I needed to be at the right time.

I believe that the events of our lives happen to prepare us for what is coming down the road along our life path, although we often don't know why until we take additional steps along that path. That's the way it has been for me.

I was hired at the Tribal School to replace an English teacher who had left in the middle of the year. There had been friction. She had insisted on teaching Native American stories as myths. But I didn't see the world that way. I had personal experience. My education had taught me that perception is reality. I taught Native American stories, not as myth, but as life.

This book is based on conflict that occurred on the Bad River Reservation in 1994 when Anishinabe Ogichidaa, or original people warriors, blockaded Wisconsin Central railroad tracks that crossed the Bad River Reservation to prevent a trainload of sulfide from going through. The sulfide would be used for mining in Michigan's Upper Peninsula.

A few years after the incident, while I was working as editor of the tribal newspaper, the Anishinabe Ogichidaa asked me to write a book about the incident.

I'm not sure this book is what they had in mind. I think they were interested in a historical account. Instead, I wrote about my experiences while on a life path that made up ten years of my life, set in the time of the railroad blockade. This book includes many stories and information, interwoven, that many people told me while I worked for the tribe. Often those stories touch upon a concept the tribe, in fact, all Native American communities have been battling for hundreds of years – the assumption of assimilation.

It was the assumption of assimilation, the idea that Native Americans should simply walk away from their culture and be assimilated into the mainstream, that has lead to conflicts over the centuries, and to major recent conflicts. When protests in Wisconsin by anti-treaty protestors in the 1980s led to horrific demonstrations at boat landings, the protestors felt justified by the weight of their assumptions. They saw treaty rights as a special right for a specific cultural group of American citizens. The protestors ranks were swelled by those who wanted to reserve the resources for themselves, and outright bigots, but the justification for all was the assumption of assimilation.

The railroad blockade in 1994 began when two Anishinabe Ogichidaa saw a vision, during a sweat, of a train carrying sulfide derailing and plunging into the Bad River, killing plants, animals, people and the sacred wild rice sloughs. The vision didn't carry much weight with the mining company or the railroad. Although it is a common assumption in tribal culture that the ancestors give just such warnings during sacred ceremonies, the common knowledge in the mainstream culture was that individuals, even communities, should risk environmental degradation for corporate profits. The corporate interests expected the tribe to bend to interstate commerce. The Anishinabe Ogichidaa didn't see it that way. They stopped the train.

Today, the assumption of assimilation is rearing its ugly head in northern Wisconsin again with a proposed open-pit iron ore mine in the Penokee Range within the Bad River watershed. It threatens the sacred wild rice sloughs and the tribe's drinking water.

Once again, the politicians who have rammed through legislation revamping the state's environmental protection laws, have demonstrated an alarming allegiance to the concept of assumed assimilation. This time the litany is "jobs, jobs, jobs," feeding on the fears of the unemployed.

Within the Native American culture, common knowledge has a different spin. Within a cultural group that has been denied access to the mainstream economic system, the jobs theme doesn't play well.

In many religious cultures, threatening the wild rice sloughs, a foundation of Ojibwe spiritual beliefs, would be akin to mining beneath the Vatican. Again, it seems to be a concept many of those in the mainstream culture find difficult to grasp.

Threatening to pollute the Bad River community's water supply is a throwback, reminiscent of the past behaviors when Native Americans were regarded as less than human. The perspective here seems to be that Native American lives are worth less, easily sacrificed for the need for steel. Whole communities in other parts of the country who have seen their watersheds destroyed by mining can relate.

My hope is that this book will raise awareness regarding the dangers of the proposed iron mine in northern Wisconsin. Given the timely, unselfish gifts given to me in the past by tribal members, I feel this is a debt I must repay. That's also why I am donating a portion of the proceeds from the sale of this book to the Penokee Hills Education Association and the Bad River Legal Defense Fund.

Yet more than anything, I hope this books helps deepen the spiritual bonds the readers feel with the Earth. What better way to do that than to view the world through the eyes of a people who have had an unbroken relationship with the Earth for thousands of years, who did not make compromises with those beliefs that allowed their culture to drift off course. (In the mainstream culture, inventing the concept of incorporation comes to mind.)

The information and stories in this book were gifted to me by those who trusted me with their stories. I have been careful to exclude information that I was told was confidential and should not be disclosed publicly.

This story is shown primarily through the eyes of the main character, Angeline. Angeline is based on a young Native American woman who started life in an orphanage in Minnesota, and was raised in the mainstream culture by adoptive parents in a Minneapolis suburb. As the book opens, she has left Minnesota and is returning to her cultural roots to find out who she really is. I felt great empathy for the person that Angeline is based on. We spent many nights at her campfire on Madeline Island talking about her life and her struggles sinking roots in her native culture.

Like Angeline, I was on a similar journey that was just beginning, learning to see through the eyes of a culture that itself was struggling to retain its identity, becoming human, living in harmony with the Earth.

My journey helped me to deepen my bonds with the planet we live on.

The industrialized world is in deep peril. A country that has made the engines of industry first, last and only, has lost its way. It blocks the sunlight needed to live.

This is a book for those who have discovered that the sunrise isn't just beautiful, but calls out to some part of their soul in a necessary way; or for those who recycle religiously, buy green, and when that becomes routine, wonder what's next?; for those who enjoyed Dancing with Wolves, but now buy Pixar

DVDs; for those who marvel at a star-filled sky undistorted by light pollution, and grow angry when a passing plane's blinking lights disturb the scene; who lie on the edge of the beach and let the waves wash over them, not because it's a hot day, but because they are drawn in by the rhythm of the waves; who have ever surprised a wild animal in nature and made eye contact; who stopped walking on that trail the way they did religiously for years, because their schedule didn't accommodate it any more, and miss it in a way that hurts. You know who you are.

An elder woman in the Bad River Tribe, a spiritual leader in the Midaewin Lodge, once told me that we humans don't get our hearts close enough to the Earth. When you think about it, she said, even when we're standing, our hearts are still several feet from the Earth. It's not enough. We need to lie on the ground to get as close as possible.

An open-pit mine removes the top layers of dirt, digging down thousands of feet, and moving the Earth downward that much farther from our hearts.

The events in this book are a culmination of both the real and imagined and are not necessarily in chronological order. The story, in whole and in parts, was gifted to me by those who entrusted it to me. The characters were created from fragments of people who crossed my path during the gestation period of this book. Each character is created by many others as we all are in life, marked by each other as wind, water, earth and sun serve to shape each other.

Prelude

Winaboozhoo, spontaneous man according to Ojibwe tradition, is a trickster and a prankster. It is his playful demeanor that gives shape and character to the plants, animals and their world.

The Apostle Islands were formed when Winaboozhoo built a dam across Chequamegon Bay on Lake Superior's south shore to trap beavers. But the beavers broke through the dam and swam away into Lake Superior. Winaboozhoo was so vexed, he threw mud at the retreating beavers. The remnants of his dam can still be seen today (Long Island). The mud he cast at the beavers became the Apostle Islands.

Ojibwe tradition forbids speaking Winaboozhoo's name except when snow is on the ground, the customary storytelling season. To do so any other time brings Winaboozhoo to your door to play tricks on you, changing the shape of your world.

Chapter One

I. The Vision

Hutch and Brewster were huddled in the hot, moist, sweat lodge barely visible in the red glow of the hot grandfather stones.

They had known each other well for years. They weren't childhood buddies. They were from different tribes. They hadn't met until they were both adults. But they had met well, became fast friends, and had walked the same path all their known lives. They called each other 'brother.'

They shared similar personalities but different coping techniques. They were both passionate men, but where Hutch practiced self-restraint, Brewster said exactly what he felt, when he felt it and loudly. It worked for both of them. When Hutch bit his lip and tightened his jaws to hold in the words, the same words came out of Brewster's mouth.

They regularly sweated together. They invited others to join them, especially recovering alcoholics or those wanting to learn about the traditional path, but Hutch and Brewster were the heart and soul of these sweats.

The lodge was located at the old pow-wow grounds, as opposed to the new one. The new one was nicer and had better facilities, but this was the traditional pow-wow grounds in the flood plain of the Bad River, under the shadow of the ancient willows that lined the river's banks, in the heart of Old Odanah.

Old Odanah was the original village on the Bad River Reservation. The old Catholic Church, St. Mary's, was nearby. The old St. Mary's School was just a few hundred yards or so from where Hutch and Brewster now sat naked on the earth. Most of Hutch's generation had been educated at that school. Then, after the school shut down, the building was used as the tribal Administration Building.

But Old Odanah was in the flood plain and once a year or so the old school basement flooded, making it difficult during high water to even get to the parking lot. Files were stored in the attic, not the basement.

And the building was contaminated — migrating toxins seeping from the old American Can Company landfill downstream. Who knew what they put in that landfill? Well, they knew. There were still monitoring wells on the site. People who were supposed to know said it wasn't a threat anymore, but tribal members living near Old Odanah, or close to the old landfill, hell, even in Diaperville, just down the road, developed cancer at higher rates than the rest of the tribe. No one on the Reservation drank the well water. The Tribe provided free water in big blue bottles in most houses and public buildings. Well, it was clean water and the bottles were good for other things, like collecting pennies.

But, for all of that, this was still the best place for a sweat lodge. There was the river, and there were the underground rivers – hidden rivers that flowed from here to there beneath ground, unseen. Water – some powerful and visible, some deep and hidden and every emotion in between – characterized this place. That's why so many of the ancestors chose to be buried near here. That's why the Catholic Church, famous for usurping tribal beliefs, had built its church and school here. That's why Hutch lived in a house just across the road. This is where the ancient spirits lived and always would.

Earlier that day, Hutch and Brewster had built their fire over the grandfather stones, had prepared the sweat according to tradition, had put a helluva a lot of work into it … Yet, he and Brewster were the only ones here now. *Oh, well*, he thought, *like we say on the Rez', "Those who are supposed to be here know who they are."*

Undeterred, he and Brewster had welcomed the ancestors and voiced their concerns, asked the spirits for blessings, even for those absent, but mostly Hutch worried.

Yeah, he was a veteran of the sun ceremony and a warrior in the good way, but he was also a worrier. He was the mother hen of a brood whose individuals were often just one step removed from alcoholism, one step away from jail time, caught in the fear of encroaching diabetes or heart disease, or berating themselves for not loving a wife or husband enough, or too much … He and Brewster had asked for blessings on all of them and even though they were the only ones here, it was still a long list. Sometimes Hutch remembered to ask a blessing for Brewster who had recently found out he was in the early stages of diabetes. He almost always forgot to ask anything for himself. Brewster took care of that for his brother.

After adding medicine to the glowing Grandfather Stones, seeing the lights of the spirits in the air, he closed his eyes. That's when it happened – the vision.

When it had passed, he opened his eyes and looked at Brewster. He didn't have to ask. He could see it in his friend's face. Brewster had seen the same thing. There was trouble coming. They would have to do something and it wouldn't be easy.

Chapter Two

I. Repercussions

The sun shined hard on Madeline Island, hard enough to threaten the memory of the glaciers that had carved the Island and left behind the surrounding puddle called Lake Superior. That's what the early French trappers and traders had named it. To the Ojibwe Tribe it was Kitchi-Gami.

It was a perfect day, the Rev. Olson thought, for a game of croquet. His children and grandchildren, fifteen in all, were visiting for the long Memorial Day weekend. What better way to fall back into the slower pace of another time than by playing a 19th century game as the 21st century loomed?

The Rev. Olson lived in a neat, wood-frame house on the southern shore of Madeline Island. His small, but faithful, Methodist congregation provided the house. The Creator provided the Island.

Madeline Island, located off the northern shore of Wisconsin, under Lake

Superior's influence, was a kind of outpost. That's the way the Rev. Olson saw it. Although a tourist attraction in the summer, the Island, fourteen miles long, had fewer than two hundred year-round residents brave enough, or dysfunctional enough, to suffer through the severe winters for the promise of summer's long days. They lived on clean water and hope. They had mastered deferred gratification.

His congregation, like those at most small churches, held a handful of active members and a larger community who appeared for weddings and funerals.

The Rev. Olson's house sat on the site of the first Catholic Church built on the Island, a mission to convert the Chippewas, or Ojibwe as they called themselves before the Europeans slurred the pronunciation with a French lisp, it was the Ojibwe migration to Lake Superior that was told in the "Song of Hiawatha," the Rev. Olson remembered from a seminary literature class. For some reason it had stuck in his mind as if he knew it might come in handy some day. He'd slept through most of the rest of the class. That was all he'd known about the indigenous people along Lake Superior's shores before relocating here from Indiana — southern Indiana hill country — not to be mistaken for places with great lakes and Island archipelagos. He had learned a little more since moving here.

His house was located next to the Indian Cemetery. Many Native Americans who had converted to Catholicism in the mid-seventeenth century, and a few who hadn't, were buried there. They included the Island's namesake, Madeline, who had converted and taken her Christian name after falling in love with trapper and trader Michel Cadotte, nearly two hundred years ago.

The graves, some with headstones, some with iron markers, others with little wooden houses built over them, were in poor condition, mimicking the fence that surrounded the cemetery. Wild flowers and weeds, most brown and withered, grew between the graves.

The fence, on the north and east

sides, was made of wrought iron, spikes protruding from the top. The lake guarded the west. The south fence, bordering Rev. Olson's house, was mostly gone.

The ancient cemetery looked out of place beside the Island lagoon, dredged in the 1960s to build a marina now filled with sailboats of different sizes and status, from luxury yachts to small sloops, reflecting wide extremes of wealth among those who made up the Island community.

The Rev. Olson was not a wealthy man, not a prominent man, at least within the church hierarchy. He was in this outpost because he had never attracted the attention of church leaders, had never caused a stir or written a Biblical commentary, had never stepped out of line or caused repercussions. He especially avoided repercussions.

He simply enjoyed the slow pace of life on the Island. He was at home in the early twenty-first century and would have been lost serving as a missionary in the 1600s. The Victorian era would have been more to his liking.

The Victorian era — with ladies in long dresses, wearing elegant hats, casually swinging croquet mallets as they strolled across the lawn. In his mind, he could see them now in summer white — elegant and cultured. But, when he blinked, he saw his own daughters, daughters-in-law and granddaughters wearing jeans and cut-off shorts with baseball caps that promoted the Green Bay Packers or Lite Beer. No long dresses. No elegant hats, but at least they could play croquet. He'd seen to that.

The yard between his house and the Indian Cemetery was the only nearby plot large enough for a croquet field. Although the property line's exact location was a hazy concept in his mind, if they were careful to stay away from the marked graves, he supposed, there would be no repercussions.

He gathered a few grandchildren to help him set the wickets and stakes while his wife and one daughter retreated into the house to make lemonade. They would need massive quantities of lemonade.

The Rev. Olson was merciless, by his own admission, when it came to croquet. He would roll up his shirtsleeves. He would work up a healthy sweat. He would play to win. Show no mercy; expect none in return. Then, at least for one afternoon, he could pretend they lived a hundred years ago when life was genteel.

The players ranged in age from the patriarch, now nearing sixty, to his youngest grandson, eight years old. They were each other's favorites, though with nearly opposite personalities. Where the Rev. Olson was a reserved conformist, the child was precocious and flamboyant. The boy brought out the child in his grandfather.

By the luck of the draw, the Rev. Olson took the first swing. His favorite grandson followed. The pair battled each other through the first few wickets before the child's red ball, following a deft swing, nudged the older man's blue ball. The child demanded his right to send the patriarch's wooden ball "for a ride." The boy lined the two balls up, side-by-side, placed his foot on top of the red sphere, practiced his swing several times, then slammed the mallet with a sharp crack! The Rev. Olson's ball shot away like this was a collision in a particle-collider and the results were experimental, not predictable.

The ball bounded off toward the cemetery, struck a fallen headstone, and landed somewhere in the middle of the neighboring property.

"Well, no problem. We can set this right," the Rev. Olson said cheerfully.

To the Rev. Olson, there was no problem that couldn't be set right, usually with a warm smile and sincere apology. He strode into the cemetery where the bright blue ball rested in a depression between mounds of earth covered with deep dried grass and wildflowers. He leaned over, despite his portly girth, and picked up his ball, then stood straight and turned.

He couldn't have been more surprised to find himself facing a young, blond woman, her nipples, unimpeded by a bra, nearly touching his ample abdomen. He could see the balance of her breasts with a quick glance down the front of her loose, soiled, minimalist, formerly white, tank top T-shirt. Exercising extreme willpower, he looked up to her face and saw the kind of grime that takes days of sleeping in cars, boats, or men's beds, far from shower facilities. Her dirty blond hair was matted and pressed against her head. He knew showers were a premium on the Island, almost a cottage industry, but this face had not been threatened by soap and water for weeks.

Her eyes were wide and wild. They gripped his eyes like a pair of discount contact lenses.

Then she spoke, turned and left.

The Rev. Olson had never before received a message from a higher source. He'd never anticipated it would happen to him. He'd never lain awake at night imagining what the messenger would look like, had never longed to be a vessel of the truth. As for truth, the truth was he'd lived his life to avoid such truths.

They were hard work, required a strength he'd never had and usually disrupted a manageable life.

But this time there was no doubt in his mind, especially as he glanced through the bushes deeper into the cemetery grounds and saw a face glaring at him, a man's face, unmistakably Indian, scowling at him in anger, making him feel weak, and making his life seem suddenly unmanageable.

He blinked and the face was gone.

Then he knew. There would be repercussions.

II. Equilibrium

Nobody knew where she lived and she liked it that way. Some people thought they did but they didn't, not really. Really, she moved around a lot. That way she could do her job and her job wasn't easy

She was the one who made sure the Island maintained its balance. That's why she slept in different places at night

— so even with her slight weight - barely a hundred pounds — she could tip things one way or another to balance it all out.

Of course, it wasn't all a matter of weight. There were other things that had to balance out, too — love and hate, anxiety and calm, intoxication and sobriety, sanity and awareness.

She did her part.

When hate grew too strong, she loved. When sobriety held sway, she got drunk. When sanity had control, she slipped over to the other side. She was normally stressed all the time.

But something was terribly wrong now. She knew it in the early morning as she slipped out of an unlocked sailboat cabin before sunrise. She sometimes slept in untended sailboats, sometimes in condominiums when she knew the resident would be spending the night elsewhere, knew because she'd witnessed him surrender to the call of pheromones, had seen him depart in his car, or hers, leaving his, or hers, behind in the parking lot. It was an Island tradition. When the bars emptied only half the cars went home for the night. The other half were picked up in the morning. She knew where most of the condo keys were hidden, the annual vacation plans or time-share schedules. Failing that, she knew which cars were usually left unlocked or which sand beaches were the most isolated, or ... If you hide out in the bathroom in one of the bars until after closing and everyone leaves, you can find a piece of floor to lie on.

But last night she slept in a sailboat, a thirty-eight foot luxury boat with mahogany trim and brass fittings inside. It was her favorite. Especially the name: Equilibrium. But there wasn't any equilibrium this morning. She could sense it as she climbed up to the fresh air and the still starlit sky.

Throughout the morning, as the sun climbed and the chill air warmed, she tried everything she knew to restore the balance. She tried meditation. She took a nap on the beach, sleeping on her right side when she usually slept on her left. She gave a hand-job to the dishwasher at the Island Restaurant and then asked him for sour food (to balance the sweet). Nothing worked. It wasn't getting better. It was getting worse.

She felt like a failure. It was her job and, even though sometimes she didn't like it, if she didn't maintain the balance who would?

By the afternoon it became apparent. There was only one thing left to do. She had to tell someone.

That's why she went to the cemetery. That's why she waited until a croquet ball rolled near her hiding place. She picked out the fat man with almost no hair because she thought at least he couldn't chase her, wouldn't hit her, or wouldn't want a hand-job.

"There's a big imbalance coming. Watch out."

She thought he understood her. She could never tell for sure when people understood her or not, but she thought he understood. She probably should have told him to 'pass it on,' but she didn't think of it. They couldn't expect her to think of everything.

Chapter Three

I. The Long Journey Home

Angeline had a relationship with her car. She was a sympathetic person with a pathetic mode of transportation. She projected her personality on her car, knew it, and didn't care what anyone else thought about it. Her car was just like her - mostly reliable, except during times of personal crisis — and it showed every hard mile driven.

Though an objective observer could still guess the original color, the car was decaying, losing micrometers of metal daily to oxidation. Angeline hardly noticed and easily forgave the mostly chartreuse Suzuki subcompact hatchback.

She, and her Suzuki, were racing along a two-lane highway in route from Minneapolis to the Apostle Islands with enough reckless abandon to set in motion a concert of familiar rattles from her car's superstructure. Lake Superior was in sight, coursing between her and the nearby Islands rising from an early morning haze.

She was surrounded by the trappings of her life, her car stuffed with her mobile nest: tent and poles, bedding, baskets, pots and pans, clothing whose patterns ranged from the outrageous to the slightly less outrageous – books, bottles, sketch pads, pencils – Oh, and candles, lots of candles, smudge pots, and lanterns. She could never have enough different ways to make fire.

She carried her rings on her fingers, and one on her toe, a toe that emerged naked through her sandal straps. The rings told the story of her life.

There was the beaded ring on her right hand. It had a matching partner her favorite niece wore on the same finger. Beside it was the silver ring with "PAX," the Latin word for "peace." Of course, there had to be a "Save the Planet" ring, just because the planet needed saving in so many ways. She still wore her wedding and engagement rings from the last time she almost got married but didn't. The decision was mutual, the decision to abandon the whole idea and stay friends. Those rings rode her third finger, wrong hand. Then, on her left hand she wore the ring given to her by an elderly woman in a Minneapolis nursing home where Angeline had worked a few years earlier. She kept it because, it seemed to her, the woman had perfected her life. What a stunning realization for Angeline: Even if we can't collectively perfect life, each of us can perfect our life, she now believed, after watching this tiny Irishwoman verbally chastise, with a truck driver's vocabulary, the world for its shortcomings. The woman had been prone to assail anyone who obstructed her appointed path, whether that appointed path was the hope of sleeping on clean bed sheets or a desire for strawberry cheesecake instead of green Jell-O for dessert. When her life was out of balance she knew how to restore it. Angeline wore the ring as a reminder that such things were possible.

She also wore an aluminum ring given her by another woman Angeline had met on a pizza delivery job — the last cottage on the lake road. She could find the house in her dreams and sometimes did. It had been Angeline's last stop every Friday night for several months. A former resort owner in the days when resorts rented little individual cabins and had names like, "The Pines Inn," or "Safe Havens." The woman had sold the rest of the property and lived in what was left of the office. Always dressed in flannel shirts and blue jeans, she only asked about Angeline and never talked about herself while they sat and ate pizza with mushrooms and black olives, sipping from brandy snifters. The woman asked honest questions, inviting honest answers and never judged her. That was important to a child abandoned at birth to a Catholic orphanage and adopted by a middle-aged, northern European couple from a Minneapolis suburb. This woman had been almost diametrically opposite of the Irishwoman, and had compromised with life years earlier, having found a satisfying, comfortable place to exist. Between the two of them, the ladies seemed to achieve a kind of balance, as if it was their mission in life to harmonize with each while completely unaware of the other's existence.

There were other rings on nearly

every finger and thumb. She wore a gold ring on one toe, a ring left behind in the restroom at a restaurant where she'd worked in Minneapolis the previous winter. She wore it in trust until she found the owner again, confident the rightful owner would return some day and claim it. And, of course, there was a silver ring she wore on a chain around her neck that depicted two dolphins swimming in opposite directions. The effect was a balance.

There were some rings she'd just bought for herself thinking the color was right, or the stone was perfect, for that time in her life. For her, they depicted entire eras. She left one thumb and one finger uncovered, and she still had nine toes for life left to live.

She wore the gift from her parents, complete with her birthstone, the sapphire, on her left hand. She'd stopped wearing that one for awhile, for years, after her father had died and her relationship with her mother, her adoptive -mother, had turned stormy. She started wearing it again only after realizing she didn't have to have it all figured out, not yet anyway. Her parents had loved her the best they could, though they hadn't much talent for it.

She eased her Suzuki onto a turn-off at a historic marker and rolled to a stop, the sound of fresh gravel, the stones formed beneath the slow wavelengths of alternately advancing and retreating glaciers, crunching beneath her tires. As she stepped out of the car she could feel the wind tossing her single braid of black hair, whipping the beaded tails of the leather thong she used to tie it back. The wind off the lake rippled the loose cotton Afghan pants, making the splashy, bright colors blur into a whirlwind of color.

She didn't look at the historic marker. She knew the words. She'd seen them in her dreams where they would always be burned into her memory. This was the type of historic marker with large yellow letters painted over a dull brown backdrop. It explained, in the appropriate cultural bias of the day, that the distant land mass was called Madeline Island, the largest of the Apostle Island chain. It was named after Equaysayway, White Crane's daughter, who had converted to Christianity two hundred years earlier, had married a French trader, and changed her name. It was understood, in Disney tradition, that she had lived happily ever after.

"What bullshit! More like, they were all driven off the Island by escalating property values and rising taxes."

She felt the anger glowing in her face. Other choice invectives came to mind and she was about to utter a few when something in the distance caught her eye — a whirlwind, or water spout, moving irregularly across the bay. It changed direction erratically, like something blind and relying on extrasensory fields to guide it, or like an erect penis attached to a freshman Congressman, relying more on dumb luck than passion. She watched with fascination until the waterspout found a definite path, directly at her. Normally, in her life, fear had been a great motivator. It sorted out her priorities. She knew the shortcut to her sense of urgency. The sign on that door read "panic." But this time she couldn't move.

The funnel of wind suddenly surrounded Angeline, throwing dust from the gravel parking area into her face, whipping her black hair, her braid, and her multi-colored afghan pants. Reflexively, she closed her eyes and raised her arms to cover her head. The bits of stone bit into her skin, and molecules of water followed to wash away the grit. Then the whirlwind was gone. She rubbed her eyes before daring to open them again.

"What was that all about?" When no one answered her rhetorical question she formed her own theory. There had to be some source of energy and, of course, nothing happens purely by accident. Was it a message meant for her?

Messages from the universe were so vague that way, she thought, feeling her level of annoyance rise. With it, the wind gusted almost in direct ratio. She decided to test her theory, reading once again the fairy tale ending to the historical marker, felt her anger rise and was once again engulfed in swirling, dust-bearing winds, this blast stronger than the last. OK, she conceded. She was the cause. The wind was drawing energy from pent-up frustrations, a few radical molecules of anger, and the fears both had drawn strength from over the years.

This time, when she opened her eyes, she avoided reading the familiar script on the marker. Instead, she shaded her sharp, black eyes to see across the water to the distant Island. Then she closed her eyes. In her mind she could see herself flying over the water, so close she could feel the cool air and smell the moisture, and then feel the sand beneath her feet as she landed on the far shore. That's where she would spend the summer, working as a waitress in a mid-scale restaurant that catered to tourists, a restaurant appropriately named, "The Restaurant."

She enjoyed waitressing — most of the time. It paid the bills and made part-time studies in art at community colleges possible. She knew the pragmatic line: 'You can't make a living as an artist,' but you can make a living as a waitress while you learn your art.

This wasn't her first trip to the Islands. Her parents had taken her camping often as a child in the Lake Superior basin. But they'd also taken her camping in less alluring locations, places that did not call her back. Madeline Island called her back, despite ghosts from the past, or at least one spirit in particular who still haunted her. She remembered the day she first met him, the scene playing out before her eyes against an Island backdrop.

II. Makwa

A 1966 Pontiac Bonneville cruised along a highway underlining Lake Superior's southern shore. Lyndon Johnson was president. The war in Vietnam was being won. The war on poverty had just begun.

The car protected its passengers from the threatening world shooting past outside like a nature video on fast-forward. The Pontiac's heavy frame and independent suspension smoothed the rough cuts from ancient glaciers that had scarred the earth's smooth skin thousands of years earlier. Airflow ventilation moderated the heat of the day. Deep cushioned seats negated both gravity and centrifugal forces.

The mother, the dominant personality in the car, sat in front on the passenger side with a road map folded across her lap. She wore a flowered, sack dress, standard issue for the era's mothers whose bodies had been re-shaped by childbirth's ordeal, mothers who had brought their children into the world guided by a family of post-modern painkillers, who had surrendered to life in a series of small compromises, who had told themselves they enjoyed time spent with the *Reader's Digest* while their husbands played poker at the VFW Hall and talked about real wars, these wives who had made "Valium" a household word. This mother wore the uniform, read the *Reader's Digest,* went to church faithfully, sometimes missed confession and felt guilty enough about the omission afterward to include it in her next confession. Unlike her contemporaries, she did not know morning sickness, feel-good hormones, a womb ripening from the conjunction of her egg and her husband's seed, and the pain of childbirth. Her brown hair was cut short to make it manageable. Evenly distributed gray hairs sprouted among the brown as if self-imposed stress had been a regular part of her life-long routine.

The father drove, smiling to himself the way some married men do when they have an excuse to focus on the task at hand and tune out their families. He wore a bowling jacket with the name of his favorite lanes stitched across both front and back. There was a slight scar on the back of his hand, the only reminder from fighting inside Germany's borders. He stared fixedly at the road as if his mantra was the drone of rubber on asphalt and the rhythmic thump of the tires striking creases in the highway's surface. His blond hair showed no trace of grey and his face displayed few wrinkles as if it had always been his wife's job to worry for herself, her husband, and adopted children.

A boy of ten years, his head covered with blond hair, testimony of an ethnic Minnesota Scandinavian background, sat between the two. He was neither held down by a seat belt nor discomforted by the protruding buckles characteristic of later model cars. *Boys Life,* a magazine read at the time by thousands of future Eagle Scouts and a few future disgruntled postal workers, covered his knees, knees scarred by collisions with newly formed suburban concrete sidewalks, the concrete still fresh and uncured.

A young girl, seven years old, slept on the wide back seat, her short, straight, black hair and dark complexion told stories about her and spoke of an ethnic background different from her family. She hugged a stuffed bear while a plastic baby doll with over-teased blond hair lay neglected on the floor beside her. A Norwegian quilt, won at a church raffle, surrounded her in rumpled folds. Her small, wiry body adjusted restlessly to uneasy sleep, her arms and legs moving in concert to her dreams.

Looking up from her map, the mother intoned a familiar, “Hm,” pointing to the side of the road, using signals the married couple, now in their forties, had cultivated through the decades. The car slowed and turned off the highway onto a side road.

The young girl didn't see any of this, not with her eyes anyway. Her small body's sense of balance registered the fact the car had slowed and changed direction. Her eyelids, pressed tightly shut, twitched repeatedly. Research in later years would disclose her sleep was in a deep REM state. Her arms moved slightly as if fending something away Her legs moved just enough to suggest running.

She awoke suddenly, her hands grabbing at the air as if the method could pull her into a sitting position. She rubbed her eyes and slowly oriented body and mind. She had dreamed she was riding in the back seat of the car and sitting next to her was an old man with long white hair tied back into a braid. He wore clothes made from animal skins and furs with colorful porcupine quill beads stitched into them, not the glass beads that followed the Europeans' arrival on North America's shores. His face was wrinkled like an apple when the skin has been peeled away and the apple is left to dry in the sun. When she looked at him, he smiled in return like a grandfather would greet a favorite grandchild. That's when she woke up.

She pushed herself upright, the heavy quilt falling away from her shoulders. She could hardly see anything outside the car. Dust swirled around them the way it did when the car was flying down a gravel road.

“Are you sure we went the right way, Harold?” the woman asked her husband, annoyed. The little girl could hear the crinkling sound of paper as her mother anxiously consulted the map.

“We’ll know soon enough,” the little girl’s father answered with the kind of patient tone that said, ‘We’re no more lost than usual for human beings.’

At that moment the car stuttered and shuddered, the engine stopping. Slowly it rolled as far as its momentum would carry it.

“Now what?” the woman muttered as if she’d expected this, or something equally bad, to happen.

As the Bonneville rolled to a stop, the little girl's view improved as the swirling dust settled around them. They'd been delivered to a place surrounded by woods and water.

To her right were thick stands of trees, an unmoving, yet ominous, presence that clung to the side of a hill and rose upward to exposed red cliffs that seemed suspended above the tree line.

On the other side of the car the land fell away to a small lake with trees crowded near the lakeshore, some reaching into the shallows with exposed roots that held them suspended above the water like the multiple legs on an octopus. Lily pads extended from the shore into the lake's placid, mirror-like water.

As the little girl's mother rolled down her window, the child could hear the chirping sounds of birds and insects instinctively searching for mates. Her father vainly tried to restart the car, the engine's moan mimicking the bird and insect calls as if the Bonneville, too, was reverting to nature.

"Now what do we do?" the child heard her mother ask, a mother vexed, it seemed, because reality had invaded their climate-controlled journey into the wilderness. The little girl's father answered by opening his car door and climbing out. Once his feet were planted on the ground, he stretched his long, lean Norwegian body, shaking out the kinks from a day of driving. The two children took their cue from him and scrambled out of the car as if compelled to meet adventure halfway.

"Michael, Angeline, come back here!" their mother commanded.

They ignored her and used their father as a shield in case she tried to press the point. Their mother reluctantly followed, glancing suspiciously at a natural world that didn't conform to her suburban sense of order. Once outside, she pulled the two children, against their inclinations, in front of her to protect her from nature's unpredictable forces.

The children, excited by the new world so different from their

Minneapolis suburb, broke away. The woman, as if suddenly stripped naked, covered her pelvis with her hands.

"I'll have to walk back," Harold said "It shouldn't be far, Gerti. I saw a bar a few miles back."

"Where are we?" she wanted to know.

"There's a sign," her husband said, pointing to a post at an intersection of two forest roads some fifty feet further down the road. It looked like most city street signs on an iron pole, but leaning south, away from dominant winds.

They walked together toward the sign, Angeline leading the way, skipping ahead, followed by her father and brother, Gerti lagging behind.

The name of the road was an Indian word none of them could pronounce.

"How do you say that?" Harold asked, turning to his wife. "Wina ... Wina ..."

"Wina-boo ..." Gerti struggled

with the word, trying to make it fit her northern European-American phonetic heritage.

"Winaboozhoo." Angeline was just as surprised as the rest of the family to hear the word flow so easily from her mouth.

"Well, now we know and you know what to tell the tow truck driver," Gerti said, reclaiming her place in the family pecking order, a role less like an alpha female and more like an executive secretary.

Harold peeled off his bowling jacket, slung it over his shoulder and unceremoniously turned back down the dirt road. He didn't have to be told twice. He recognized an escape route from a demanding family when he saw one.

As he faded into the dust settling along the road behind them, the two children wasted no time finding a path that led around the lake and into the woods.

"Angeline! Michael! No! You stay here until your father gets back," their mother insisted, chasing the two children with halting steps. Michael stopped as if he understood this time he was the one who got caught. Angeline kept going.

"Angeline," her mother's distant voice called out to her. "Your heart!"

Racing down the path like a laboratory animal who'd found the cage door left unlocked, she ran until she didn't fear recapture, then stopped and listened. She heard laughter, ahead and further down the path, and felt attracted to it the way smelt, a finger-length fish, are drawn by the billions to Lake Superior's shores each spring to spawn.

She saw something move, rustling leaves beside the path. Two tiny men leaped onto the path near her feet, one about three feet small and the other about half that size. Too surprised to be scared, she watched as the tiny figures jumped up and down in front of her, waving their arms. She was about to reach out and touch one when he spoke.

"Whatever you do don't go that way," the larger one said, pointing down the path in a high-pitched voice like the wind forced through a crack in a glacier.

"Not that way!" the smaller one shouted in a deep voice like wind lost in a cave.

Being a child, her instinct was to do the opposite of what she was told. She giggled and disobeyed, running on, compelled. At those moments when she stopped to rest, feeling discouraged, the dancing, laughing voice would entice her again, this time joined to a face, a glimpse, a shadow of the old man who'd sat next to her in her dream in the back seat of the Bonneville. He laughed at her and ran ahead into the brush, propelled by surprisingly spry legs. She hurried after him.

When she became worried she might be lost, she again caught sight of the old man darting around a large rock formation. She ran to keep up, focusing so completely on her pace she was caught entirely off-guard when she burst through rock pillars and found herself face-to-face with a large black bear. No more than three feet away, he stood solidly on four legs, barring her path. She felt his breath on her face. She felt her heart racing. The bear extended his head forward, sniffing at her, as if trying to decide if she was from his world or another. He leaned toward her, drawing a delighted laugh from the old man, seated on a rock ledge above and behind them. He laughed out loud. The bear sniffed at her again, this time so close she could smell his breath.

"Makwa!" the old man said. The bear turned as if recognizing his name. "Gotigobide!"

The bear snarled, resisting the command. "Gotigobide," the old man repeated firmly. The bear turned away and left, ambling into the brush. The old man climbed down from his perch and approached the little girl until he stood where the bear had been. He sniffed, then smiled. "Gichi-mookomann?" he said, pointing at her. "Gichi-mookomann?" Then he shook his head side-to-side and smiled, smiled as if he would now give her the truth about herself.

"Anishinabe." This time his finger touched her heart as he spoke.

"Anishinabe."

Then he bounded away, following the same path broken by the bear.

III. Taking Heart

Of course, he would touch her heart. Angeline thought, still staring across the water at the Island, her Suzuki idling beside her. It was as if he knew instinctively where she hurt the most. Her heart. … the cause of so much anguish in her life.

"Be careful, Angeline, you're heart," her mother had told her thousands of times when she tried to run, or jump, or play, or just be a normal, happy child. She'd been born with a heart murmur. That was the physical side of it, but the ailment was more than a cruel trick of fate.

She didn't know her real mother, except maybe as a heartbeat from the womb when the day's stress laid Angeline to sleep at night in the fetal position and she could hear the distant echoes from the womb. Didn't know her real father, or anything about him, except that he was Indian. She didn't know which tribe. The orphanage administrators claimed the records were lost. Who knew for sure? The company line at that time was that it was better for the adopted child to forget and move on. Her mother was a carnival worker, they said. She'd given Angeline over to a Catholic orphanage in Minneapolis immediately after birth, where Angeline had spent her first year of life. She couldn't remember anything about it, except a few strangely familiar smells, or sounds she bumped into at odd times during the normal course of life, like the smell of antiseptic cleaners or the deep echoes of prayer. That was it, the sum and total. No wonder her heart stammered and stuttered. No wonder —

Her thoughts were interrupted by the noise of an oncoming eighteen-wheeler, and the subsequent after tow of wind that pulled against her, urging her down the highway.

She rubbed the dust from her eyes, and climbed back into her Suzuki, aiming toward the ferry dock. The traffic was heavy and the line of vehicles at the dock was backed into a snake-like maze of cars, trucks, and RVs, overloaded with vacation gear as if they really could take it all with them. What was the point of getting away... She boarded with the Memorial Day weekend tourists, her subcompact sandwiched between a bulky RV and a Mercedes convertible with the top up. What a waste, she thought, to have a convertible and not drop the top on a day like this.

A group of cyclists, with helmets, Spandex and defined thighs and abs, crowded their French-made mountain bikes into an open space in front of her. Still, through that forest of lightweight alloys, she could see the Island across the channel, her view occasionally interrupted by a shapely mainsail from a sloop-rigged sailboat, heeled to the gunwales, cutting across the ferry's intended path.

She closed her eyes as the ferry pulled away from the dock, her bodily fluids flowing in rhythm to the waves, her thoughts drifting. She'd tried finding

Winaboozhoo Road once, to return to that magical place, a few years earlier — just a weekend trip. She decided to ask directions at one of those corner bar-store-and-gas-stations. After all, she wasn't a man. She could ask directions and not feel her self-identity was threatened.

There were two doors. She picked the one that looked more like the gas station, though as thirsty as she was from her long, dusty drive, she wouldn't have been disappointed to find the bar instead.

Inside,, two men, one white, wearing greasy coveralls, his blond hair almost as greasy, and an Indian in a black T-shirt and jeans with his long black hair tied back in a pony tail, sat in chairs beside a small table. The table held two coffee cups, a grease gun, and a chessboard, the game already in progress. Half-eaten donuts threatened to spill out of their box onto the grease gun.

"Maybe you can help me," she began. "I'm looking for a road. I was on it years ago when I was a child. I think it's around here somewhere, but I'm not sure."

"What's it called?" the greasy blond answered cheerfully, putting down his donut.

"Winaboozhoo Road." The two men looked at each other, confusion crossing their faces.

"Never heard of it, you?" the white man said, looking at the Indian as if deferring to his expertise.

"No such thing," the Indian said.

Angeline didn't mean to question them, but of course there was. Maybe it existed in the Twilight Zone, or only showed up to confuse the tourists who drove by in their Pontiac Bonnevilles, but it was out there somewhere. She knew it then and she knew it now, the same way she'd known she was different from her Scandinavian and German parents, the same way she'd known her life was on a different road. She just knew.

She'd always known certain things. Scared the hell out of her mother sometimes, like the time when she told her mother that the priest was coming to visit them that night. “No, the priest isn’t coming to visit,” her mother had insisted. “You’ll see,” Angeline had told her. Later that night someone knocked on their door. When her mother opened it and saw the priest standing there, she immediately turned and directed an icy stare at her daughter. They did not speak of it again.

There was another time, another vacation, when they were all driving down another highway in that same Bonneville, Angeline asleep in the back and she had that nightmare, about a terrible storm, the wind hurling sticks across the highway and shoving the car back and forth on the road and then a wall of water crashing down on them, lifting the car and carrying it toward the lake, toward angry waves churning the brown silt from its bed, and —

She awoke screaming. Her mother carefully folded the map — there was always that map on her lap — and reassured Angeline that there was no storm. “See? The sun is shining.” Still, they had to pull over to the side of the road and it took a full ten minutes before Angeline felt secure enough to stop crying.

But there was a storm, it swirled down on them not thirty minutes later, forcing her father to slow down or risk losing control in the sheets of rain that poured on them. A roadblock, with flashing red lights and police in yellow rain slickers, stopped them.

"How far you going?" the policeman asked, once her father had rolled down his window.

"Another hour, maybe," her father answered.

"You should be OK. But you're lucky. Ten minutes earlier and you'd have been washed off the road." The policeman nodded toward the ditch where the water had washed away a portion of the road, leaving a gaping gully in the red earth.

Her mother had immediately turned to look back at her daughter, those same pinched lips and scowling eyebrows. They never spoke of that again, either.

IV. Rough Landing

Angeline, her eyes still closed, could feel the ferry slow as it slipped inside the Island breakwater and turned to approach the dock. The engines roared into reverse, braking the ferry and slowing it to a crawl. She opened her eyes in anticipation of a gentle docking. Passengers began moving about the boat, returning to their vehicles, gripping their bikes, gathering their bundles, and standing ready.

But, at the last second, the ferry lurched forward, striking the dock with enough force to tip over passengers and mountain bikes. It was uncharacteristic ferry behavior, she thought, as she replaced a campfire coffee pot on top of the stack of equipment piled in her back seat. Maybe a wave had eluded the breakwater and had pushed them into the dock. Maybe it was human error. Or maybe the Island itself had lost its balance and had stumbled into the boat while trying to recover.

Once the ferry was safely docked, Angeline debarked and drove into town, cutting through a back street on her way to the Town Park, midway across the Island, halfway between shores, where she would set up camp. She was looking for positive signs, harbingers welcoming her back to the Island, *back home,* she thought, something to balance out their rough docking.

The street took her past the open back door of The Restaurant where she would be working that summer. She thought she saw, from the corner of her eye, a fragile-looking dishwater blond furiously administering a hand-job to a dishwasher. As signs went, that was fairly compelling, but not what she was looking for.

She was looking for something, or someone specific. Of course, she didn't expect him to jump in front of her car, but ... She turned down a back street, past the museum and toward the main road, then headed in the direction of the campground. She had a tent to pitch, a fire to build, spirits to attract. This Island, the traditional cultural center of the Ojibwe tribe, had to be the place. That's why she was here, as far as she was concerned.

Well, there was one more reason, if she was being honest: To face a demon from her past — a fear, really. It had happened six years earlier, her first trip back to the Island without her parents. She'd set up camp in the Town Park. She'd felt relaxed, at home, after a long day in the sun sketching waves crashing against the rocky north shore, and a night of making new friends in various cafes and bars, before falling asleep in her small tent, a few coals still glowing in her campfire. She was awakened during the night by the sound of a large animal moving around in her camp. It was a bear, she knew without looking. She knew bears. She'd seen them from close range.

It approached her tent, stood over the flimsy shelter, her head inches away with only a thin layer of synthetic cloth separating her from the angry creature. The bear growled at her, causing

Angeline's heart to race and stutter. She fought to calm herself, and somehow her heart held steady until the bear gave up and wandered off, but she didn't sleep again that night. Now she associated bears, and racing hearts, with every attempt to run away from home. Of course, she'd only run away from home that once, and this time made two. The bear had kept her from the Island for years. But the attraction proved too strong, like revisiting the midway concourse where she first learned that most carnival games are rigged. She had to come back and test this new truth. Sometimes she feared, sometimes she hoped, that she was right. She was learning that about life. In dim light, fears and hopes can look the same, when only the names have been changed.

V. The Spirit Stone

Long shadows began to form around the Madeline Island Museum as the first official tourism weekend neared its end. Unlike December, when the sun set minutes after 4 p.m. with the northern hemisphere nearing the winter solstice, the summer sun seemed to linger longer than the memory of a former lover gone, but never forgotten.

The museum curator walked around the wood-frame building's grounds, picking up the odd junk food wrapper as part of his daily ritual before closing up. Well, that and checking the restrooms to make sure there were no young blonds, dirty and slightly screwy, loitering in the hope they would get locked inside for the night.

The curator, a man in his thirties, with dark hair just beginning to thin at the temples, looked like someone who had been young and enthusiastic when first assigned to this job, but had already traded his youth for the first halting signs of maturity and grudging compromises with reality.

He breathed deeply. He could smell the moisture beginning to collect on the green grass. He glanced at the falling sun and could already see it would form into a spectacular sunset this evening.

He turned and walked familiar ground back toward the building, a path he'd taken hundreds of times over the years. He didn't even look down as he walked.

As he neared the door his foot struck something unfamiliar. He stumbled and fell.

He looked back, his eyes focusing on the Spirit Stone. Weighing nearly 200 pounds, the stone was one of the Ojibwe tribe's most powerful spiritual artifacts. Tribal members didn't refer to the stone as "it." The stone was "he," complete with his own personality. In the 1920s a tribal medicine woman saw what was happening to Ojibwe spiritual icons. They were being sold by those facing economic destitution. Tribal members, at least those who could remember a happier time, became demoralized by their culture's disintegration, or caught in the grip of advanced alcoholism, and took what they could get in cash to keep going a few more days. That would not happen to "him," the medicine woman vowed, before turning the stone over to the protection and care of the local college. From there the stone made his way to the museum. He would be safe there until the time came for his repatriation to the tribe, until his journey home.

The museum curator had passed the stone more times than he could count and not once had he ever misstepped so badly that he was forced to his knees. He crawled back to the stone, his foot numb. He wasn't sure he could brace his ankle firmly enough to walk. He ran his hand along the stone's bottom edge and found exposed dirt, the way one might find raw earth after kicking aside a rock which had been in the same place long enough to kill the grass and incubate a subculture of insects beneath. Maybe it was his imagination, but it seemed the stone had moved.

He knew he hadn't struck it hard enough to stir it. True, his foot throbbed and he couldn't move his toes, but an elephant kick might not be strong enough to influence this stone. Had someone tried lifting it? That had to be it, he decided. No stone, not even the Spirit Stone, could walk on its own.

Chapter Four

I. Rumors, Myths, Legends and Lies

On Madeline Island an entertaining lie received better play than the truth.

The Island was ripe with rumors, myths, legends, and just damn good lies though, by definition, there were no lies on the Island, only truth stretched to its outer limits. "The truth" suffered by comparison.

But truth (without the preposition) eventually evolved from these basic building blocks: legend, myth and grains of the truth enhanced by creative energies. For example, there was the truth of Tom's Burned Down Cafe.

One night, several years ago, Tom's Cafe caught fire and burned down to the floorboards. Tom, being an enterprising individual, erected a canvas tent over the flooring and renamed the cafe for the infamous night it had glowed hot enough to attract every sightseer on the Island.

Dramatic, yes, but not yet the stuff of truth.

Tom and his cousin Bernie were practicing sibling rivalists. No two Island residents stood at more extreme poles — at least among those related by the accident of birth. Tom tied his hair back in a ponytail. His cousin wore his with a razor cut and sideburns. Torn was an anarchist. His cousin was on the Town Board and regarded the pile of scrap metal left over from the fire as a blight on the town's good image. He tried to have the property condemned.

Tom had a different point of view. He looked at the pile of scrap metal and saw the raw material for sculpture. He applied for an arts board grant and used the money to bring in sculptors just to prove the point. Since he was an old hand with an acetylene torch, he even tried a few designs of his own creation, modestly deflecting any praise that came his way.

The truth, of course, is that one man's pile of junk is another man's leverage over his sibling.

Then there was myth: in the early 1960s, the Island movers and shakers asked for the help of the Army Corps of Engineers to dredge the south lagoon for a marina. No one thought to consult with either the Ojibwe tribe or a qualified historian. Either one might have predicted the outcome. An amateur historian could have told them that missionaries had a habit of usurping native customs, instead of trying to change them wholesale — bait and switch, the same way the winter solstice was replaced by Christmas once Christians moved into pagan neighborhoods. Then there was the free market's efforts to usurp Christmas in exchange for buying frenzies.

The first Catholic Church was probably built near the lagoon because it was already sacred to the Ojibwe. The adjoining cemetery was very likely built on native burial grounds. Native Americans didn't plat their cemeteries, or assign sextons to keep track of who was buried where. Once dead, both European and Ojibwe bodies broke down and returned to the earth. The difference was: Native Americans didn't pretend otherwise with headstones meant to outlast civilizations. Therefore, an amateur historian could have told the Corps that dredging near the cemetery, located hard on the shores of the lagoon, would probably unearth unmarked graves. The Ojibwe tried to tell them. No one listened.

That's exactly what happened. Most of the bones ended up in the Smithsonian Institute and the artifacts wound up in the local museum, but in that way Madeline Island was no different than the world-at-large. Human bones found in an unmarked grave must have archeological value, even if digging up a set of bones in a Christian cemetery from the same era would constitute sacrilege.

After the dredging, sightings of strange lights in the lagoon increased dramatically. Angeline could have identified the source. She had a talent for seeing things others missed, from playful childhood companions to vaporous adult houseguests, even predicting the arrival of priests.

Once, as a newly emancipated young adult, she'd shared a house in Minneapolis with a host of disassociated spirits. She'd learned a thing or two about them. There were so many in the house they became a real nuisance. Some nights the lights made sleep as difficult as finding a healthy self-esteem for a child whose early bonding stage was interrupted by the carnival circuit. The show must go on. Not all the spirits shared a history with the house. They certainly weren't trapped there. It wasn't a "haunt", so to speak. They sometimes followed her around during the day and would later give unsolicited advice about stupid mistakes she'd made. They were like family that way: annoying.

Part of the attraction, Angeline learned, was water — in this case a nearby inland lake. The spirits were attracted to the water. That was their story anyway.

And they were obsessed by sex. They encouraged Angeline, and her live-in of the time, to indulge as often as possible. Some kind of vicarious thrill was involved.

Madeline Island Marina fit the mold. There was water, of course. There was sex, if weekend sailors don't lie, at least no more than weekend fishermen.

Then there was the hotel swimming pool. Located across a narrow channel from the cemetery. The rite of passage among young summer residents meant skinny-dipping in the hotel pool without getting caught. Or, maybe getting caught was part of the thrill. What was the attraction? Maybe the youths sensed an enthusiastic spiritual audience.

Not that hedonism on the Island was restricted to the cemetery and surrounding area. But the odds were better. That's the stuff myths are made of, Angeline knew.

She wasn't sure what truth existed in that, except it's all connected somehow.

For truth-stretched-to-the-outer-limits-of-believability, Angeline had to go no further than the place where she worked.

Ben, a refugee from the political activist wars of 1960s Chicago, owned and operated The Restaurant. Unique decorating scheme would be an understatement. The decor represented schizophrenia at best, multiple personalities at worst. There was the usual debris from the 1960s: Prints from "The Hobbit", Picasso's "Guernica" and several Miro recreations. There were a few original abstracts painted by avowed friends. Like someone at ease simultaneously talking, smoking and drinking coffee, all spaces on the interior walls were busy with some display. Ben was the sort who demanded his eye to be constantly distracted. There were pictures of his wife and kids from years earlier, like someone who had tried the good life, complete with a Kodak Brownie camera, but eventually realized he had no talent for it.

Most eerie were the pictures drawn in bold crayons by kids who lived and grew up on the Island. Apparently spirits of all shapes and descriptions visited their dreams and the children, not blinded yet by society's norms, gave them shape and form. When Angeline decided to hang one of her drawings in that shadowy gallery, if looked best beside the spontaneous images captured by the Island kids.

If there were mirrors that could reflect personality instead of person, The Restaurant was Ben's dressing room mirror. It was his walk-in hell.

There was a precedent here. Ben was afraid of water. That's why he lived on an Island, he said. That way, he could keep his fears in plain sight where they couldn't sneak up on him.

For Angeline, the irony was that she fit here.

She tried living up to the dining room's reputation by wearing clothes that either complimented the room or contradicted it. Neither angle of approach was easy, not when she tried, sometimes working too hard at it. The room had a way of shifting shadow, tone and pattern, depending on who was sitting at which table, or what color the lake was that morning. Still, most days she'd match the room at least once, if only accidentally.

Today, Memorial Day Monday, the lake was a deep blue with a touch of gray. The blue said the water temperature was warming, and the angle of the sun was climbing toward the summer solstice. The grey said the water was turning over, exchanging the cold for the warm, but that it was still cold. Make no mistake. It was still cold.

Ben sat at a table with a pair of late-morning guests. Angeline had seen him do this before. He believed it was his responsibility to mingle with the customers, to socialize, to give them the full "Restaurant experience".

"I was in the eye of the storm in Chicago," he told the young couple as he puffed on his cigarette. Ben held the cigarette loosely between his first two fingers and never let his hand stray more than two inches from his mouth. He typically built a noxious cloud between himself and any listeners as a kind of self-defense mechanism. Like his liberal attitudes, his socially incorrect behavioral traits were safe from society's condemnation here. He was allowed, almost encouraged, to be an Island anachronism. His listeners, this morning, were the kind of people who didn't have the tools to defend themselves from his brand of intrusion. Some people suffered his stories silently. Some amused themselves with veiled insults. There were the rare few who were genuinely interested.

"This country has forgotten what it was like in those days. Civil rights didn't just happen. There had to be marching in the streets. There had to be confrontation with skirmish lines of cops in riot gear. There had to be a stare-down with Richard Daley. It had to happen." He waved his cigarette in the couples' faces. They suffered the smoke as if they believed some shortcoming of theirs had led them to this purgatory. The mandatory sentence was confinement through a late breakfast in Ben's walk-in hell.

"The repercussions are still being felt today," he intoned. He looked around as if undecided whether to risk pausing for a breath like someone accustomed to being interrupted every time he tried it. This time, he took a chance, thinking it was safe. Angeline watched with interest, ready to lay odds against him.

Lenny was expert at interruption. He shattered polite conversations with the skill of someone good-natured and socially unskilled – with exuberance and innocence. It was his job, when not cutting brush, delivering messages, digging holes, or riding his one-speed bicycle with great energy around the Island, to keep rumors circulating. He had an innate talent to recognize the moment a rumor was ripe. He also had a talent for entrances. He didn't enter rooms. He burst into them with wide-eyed enthusiasm. Ben made the mistake of allowing eye contact.

"Did you hear? There's a reporter down at the Indian Cemetery. There's gonna be a incident," he said breathlessly, then exited without explanation.

Angeline thought she recognized a future legend in the formative stage.

II. The Incident

The impending incident was just the excuse Ben's trapped couple needed to escape. They raced from the building. Once outside, they turned the wrong way as if more interested in a clean getaway than an Island incident. Angeline didn't correct them. Everyone else in the building who wasn't a slave to the work place, who was alive and had a natural interest in life's curiosities, also chose that moment to exit hell.

Angeline was on the time-clock and had no choice but to stay.

Ben had a choice. He didn't stir, annoyed that his unsuspecting listeners had fallen for something so trite.

"You can go after them," Angeline advised him.

"It won't be an incident until I get there," he answered.

"You need to live a little, Ben, or one of these days, when you look in the newspaper, you'll see your own obituary. It'll say, 'Died in 1969, but his heart didn't stop beating until 1994.'"

Ben frowned and then went to the kitchen to chase a dishwater blond with matted hair out of his business establishment.

Angeline was less interested in the crowd that flowed out the door than she was in the two women who were trying to enter. They didn't fight the current, but didn't retreat from it either, holding their ground and allowing the current to flow around them. One was dressed like an unrepentant transient, or as though she worried once a day about her stock dividends. On Madeline Island, it wasn't always easy to tell the difference. Her hair was short, straight and black with strands of grey. It looked like it had been cut short to make it manageable, and was neglected anyway. She had a face which appeared as if it had been exposed to the sun more years than not. Her actions were precise and confident. She chose the table where the pair would sit. She assumed that the chair she wanted would want her. She was the first to glance at Angeline as if to signal they were ready for the menus now.

The other woman had long, straight blond hair and a fair complexion that must have fought against sun exposure at every opportunity. She seemed to scan the room first before entering as if checking to ascertain if hidden dangers lurked here. Of course, they did, but most people were not as cognizant of them as this woman was. She accepted her companion's choice of tables with great reservation. When she chose a chair, it was as if she had to first convince it to bear her before she could sit down. Both were small women, both in their late 40s or early 50s, the age when women either feared the loss of their youthful appearance or stopped caring and got comfortable with themselves. These women had gotten comfortable with themselves. But those similarities aside, they were otherwise as different as politics and good intentions. It was as if, together, they struck a balance and could never wander more than a few feet from each other or both would topple over.

"Aren't you going to go see the incident?" Angeline asked as she brought the obligatory glass of water.

"Incident? What incident?" the dark-haired woman asked with a slight Germanic accent.

The guest was dangerously close to identifying herself as a tourist. But no, there was mud on her battered hiking boots. Tourists never actually touched Island soil.

"At the Indian Cemetery. You haven't heard?"

"If it's a real incident, it can wait until after I eat," she answered decisively. Her name was Ursula. She was originally from Prague, but had lived on the Island for the past five years. Glenda had arrived on the Island the same day as Ursula, but from Canada's Maritimes. Though they hadn't known each other, or of each other, before setting foot on the Island, they met here and became close friends before the sun had set that first day. Angeline liked them. They were like the Irishwoman and the pizza-stop woman from her past.

They knew each other well enough

to know they'd rather eat today than witness an incident. While Ursula threw herself into the food experience, Glenda was constantly on her guard, noting every changing circumstance, stopping in mid-bite to scrutinize each new customer who entered, if these two had been creatures of the forest, Ursula would have been the water animal basking near the shore, unconcerned about threats, real or perceived, since the water and safety were just a dive away. Glenda would have been territorial, having splashed her scent at the boundaries of ground she now felt obligated to defend. Both had a great interest in spirits, especially Island spirits, Angeline found out before she finished taking their orders.

Glenda preferred using devining devices - Tarot, Medicine Cards, I Ching ... Ursula simply communed.

They knew the place where Angeline had pitched her tent — not just the campground in general, but the exact site where she had sunk her stakes as if they had memorized every inch of the Island.

“You have any trouble with bears?” Ursula wanted to know.

“Not yet.” Angeline answered.

“Good. Let's hope they’ve accepted you. There’s a lot of spirit activity on that end of the Island – a bit darker and more depressing as if it had more tragedies to remember.”

Angeline noticed the previously trapped couple wander past The Restaurant, glancing nervously from side to side. She was about to step out front and give them directions to some safe place, when Ursula interrupted her.

“Ahem ..." She was staring at Angeline’s foot. “That’s a lovely ring on your toe.”

“Thank you,” Angeline answered, looking down as if she hadn’t noticed her own foot in a long time.

“I used to have a ring very much like that,” she commented, leaning close. “Very much like that ...”

“I found it in a restroom in Minneapolis,” she confessed, leaning down to remove it for closer inspection. "I've been taking care of it until I found the owner."

"That could be it ..." Ursula said, leaning closer still and squinting. "Which restroom?"

"If you think it's yours, you can have it back," Angeline offered. Ursula looked up into Angeline's dark eyes, as if seeing deeply into her soul for the first time.

"No, you keep it," she told the younger woman. "You've done well with it so far. Better than me. Keep it a little longer."

Angeline never doubted that the ring belonged to Ursula. Rings know their owners and send out familiar signals, she believed.

Ben returned from the kitchen, pulling on a jacket and heading toward the door.

"I'm going to the beach," he announced on his way out, turning left and striding down the sidewalk with a sense of purpose.

"Except, the beach would be the other way," Angeline said to herself, watching him go. "That way ... that would be the way to the Indian Cemetery."

Ursula's act of trust had put Angeline in a generous mood when the young dishwater blond returned to the kitchen near closing time. Angeline listened with interest to Equilibrium's theories about harmony and balance.

When Equilibrium tried to eat and run, Angeline calmed her.

"I don't expect any more customers, or bosses, not as long as there's an incident going on," she told her guest. "You wouldn't know anything about any incidents, would you?"

"I might," Equilibrium answered, trying to be coy. Angeline knew a guilty look when she saw one.

"Then, tell me about it, girlfriend."

"Well, it could be that someone who's in charge of keeping balance on the Island had a really bad day and sort of lost track of things for awhile," Equilibrium began, while intermittently eyeing the dessert tray.

"Not to mention any names."

"No, no names," Equilibrium agreed wholeheartedly. "Anyway, that someone might have thought she should tell someone else about the big imbalance coming."

"And?"

"And she might have seen someone hit a croquet ball into the cemetery, and thought, 'that could be a sign,' and then hid in the cemetery until the fat man was close enough to tell him."

"Theoretically, of course."

"Of course. And then, maybe she ran and forgot to tell him to pass it on."

"Relax, girl. I think you're off the hook. Nobody cares about a big imbalance, but a croquet ball hit into the cemetery, that's news. Have some dessert, before you get any skinnier and disappear completely."

Then Angeline fed her leftover chocolate pudding and vowed to do her part to restore the Island's balance.

III. The Prehistoric Ford Truck

On the way back to her campground home in the late afternoon, Angeline stopped at Tom's Burned Down Cafe for a shower. Tom sold beer, time in the showers, and atmosphere.

If The Restaurant was Ben's walk-in hell, then Tom's Burned Down Cafe was a free-association heaven. The two businesses balanced each other that way.

The cafe was nothing more than a platform, the remnants of the original building's floor, with a semi-truck trailer backed up to it and a canvas tent over the top, the sides exposed to the elements. The bathroom, showers and storage space were in the trailer. The showers were rented to those in desperate need of cleansing. That's where Angeline went to shower on those days when Lake

Superior was too cold to swim in, which included most of June, July and part of August.

Tom never told the same story about how his business had evolved into its present state. That would be too boring — for him anyway, but most of the time his theory of the weakest link fit into one version or another. For most people, the theory meant that no chain is stronger than its weakest link. Tom had a different interpretation.

The day after the fire, he discovered the weak link in his business — himself. He'd somehow forgotten to pay the fire insurance. Rather than hide from the fact, he publicized it. At the following Fourth of July Parade he had a sign made and affixed to the roof of his 1960s era pink Cadillac: "You've got to be tough, if you're going to be stupid." So much for the marketing phase.

As the sort of person who operated on the abstract plane, Tom realized he needed a concept before he could begin rebuilding. He spent many hours sifting through piles of charred wood and twisted angle iron before it came to him. The weak-link theory had another connotation. Since a chain is no stronger than its weakest link, there was no point in any link being any stronger than the weakest. That carried him through the rebuilding stage.

Instead of bulldozing away the debris and starting over with new parts, Tom began attaching the leftover bits and pieces together, sometimes without a notion of what the finished product might resemble. By attaching the weak links — leftover fire-scarred floorboards with tables and chairs, plumbing with wiring with a pink Cadillac — it resembled a cafe.

He discovered a corollary to his original theory. "Junk will expand to fill available space." He gave it a name and kept the doors open, so to speak, since none of the doors survived the fire.

Messages began to appear on unoccupied flat surfaces: table tops, counter tops, chairs and floor.

"A mind that expands to encompass a new idea never returns to its original size." — O. Wendall Berry. Turning back to the past was not in Tom's philosophy.

Or, "Risk. Security is mostly superstition ... it does not exist in nature. Life is either a daring adventure or nothing." — Helen Keller.

And, "The universe is not only stranger than you imagine — it's stranger than you can imagine." — Albert Einstein.

If given a choice between walking boldly through life or walking around it, Tom had made his choice.

"Only those who go too far know how far they can go," he'd etched on a tabletop. You didn't have to walk across the room to find: "Control is an illusion. Life is the ability to deal with Plan B."

That explained most of the café's early evolutionary period. Over the intervening years, other pieces were added to the puzzle, including his prehistoric Ford pick-up truck.

The prehistoric Ford was a by-product of his first sculpting workshop. The vehicle had been sitting behind the cafe almost since the beginning of time. It pre-dated the fire. It was there before Tom owned the café. Some people believed it was there before the first tourists arrived and started the Island's modern era. Future archeologists would have no trouble identifying its place in history. Obviously, it came from the Detroit basin, early fossil-fuel era. At least that's the way the artist saw it through her unique point of view. The artist had a point of view developed over many years of not fitting in anywhere else, so she fit in perfectly on the Island.

When she looked at the old Ford truck, and tried to breathe life into it, or see it as it truly was — a collection of living molecules — she saw a prehistoric creature with no natural enemies, except itself — and maybe rust. She kept the hood in place, cutting saw-toothed, razor-sharp teeth across the bottom edge. She left the headlamps to represent eyes, below the mouth and its gaping incisors. If there was a message in natural selection, this message said the creature was more interested in feeding than seeing.

She removed the truck's bed altogether. Truth be known, this was no beast of burden, not really. It placed a greater burden on those who thought they could possess it. The cab and seats had to go, too. Although it sometimes consented to passengers, there was no question who was in control. The front wheels stayed with little more than a skeleton of chassis trailing behind, giving the appearance, with severe perspective, it was lunging at you — in your face!

Tom liked it. It had a gargoyle effect sitting in front of his cafe, driving away evil spirits or things which might have escaped from nearby walk-in hells.

IV. The Unexpected Guest

Tom was always good for a different perspective, and today Angeline was interested in his point of view as she emerged from his rental shower, towel-drying her hair after a long day at work.

Yes, Tom had heard there was going to be an incident, but that it hadn't yet fully matured from a misunderstanding.

"Perception is reality," he told Angeline.

"What does that mean?" she asked.

"It won't be a real incident until the TV cameras get here."

Tom was sort of an optimistic cynic, or maybe a conservative nihilist. He didn't call himself a Republican or a Democrat. Instead, he described himself as a "Tommunist."

"It does make me wonder though. If they call that an incident, then what was the Treaty of 1854?"

Tom had a point. He almost always did, though he delighted in making you search for it. His day was complete if a one-liner got a laugh on the spot and then a time-delayed, "What the hell did he mean by that?" It occurred to her, on the drive to her campsite, there might be more below the surface of

Tom's remark. Not the one about the Treaty of 1854. That was obvious enough for a dedicated National Enquirer subscriber to catch. No, she was thinking about perception and reality. That spoke to her. She didn't know many people whose perception of reality would be seen in a public place with hers. Not many fellow human beings had walked the same path she had walked in her life, or whose view of life had been challenged so thoroughly that they were open to almost any nightmare she could share with them, and most of them lived on Madeline Island.

I'm starting to free associate, she thought. *That can't be good.* She was simply too tired to sort it out now.

She recognized her road, automatically turned the old Suzuki onto the gravel road into the campground, glanced up at the street sign, let the various brain synapses register the words, "Winaboozhoo Road" in black letters over a yellow background, allowed herself a second to react, and hit the brakes. Her synapses had been wrong before and probably would be again sometime. Could she trust what she saw? She slammed the SUV into reverse and backed up. This time when she looked up at the sign she saw "Town Park Road" in the same black letters on the same yellow background, the same post leaning away from prevailing winds.

"I'll be OK," she told herself, "as long as I don't start talking to myself." She shifted the car back into a forward gear and rolled over thinning gravel to her campsite.

There would be a chill this night, she thought, as she lit a fire. Still, it wasn't cold enough to keep away the mosquitoes, affectionately known on the Island as the Wisconsin State Bird. She preferred to think of them as nature's flying acupuncture needles. She lit her collection of smudge pots, strategically located in branches of surrounding trees, to drive away all flying things.

She stayed at her fire just long enough for the surrounding ground to absorb some of the warmth — from her and the fire. The ground, she knew, would be generous and give it back during the night.

She was ready to embrace sleep when she crawled between the blankets piled high in her tent. Instead, it was one of those nights when sleep took the form of exhaustion: Came fast and furious, and delivered a disturbing dream.

She dreamed she heard some living thing moving around her campground. It was the bear again, she thought, her heart pounding.

She opened her eyes, but instead of staring straight into synthetic nylon cloth, she had somehow acquired the ability to see through the tent walls. There was a bear all right, only it was larger than your typical Island black bear. It was as large as a Kodiak: six feet at the shoulders. She could feel the ground shake as the wild animal snuffed around her campground. When it turned to face her, his eyes locked onto hers. Yet when it opened its mouth it wasn't to growl, but to speak.

"You don't need to be afraid of me anymore," he told her in a voice that rumbled, a voice she could feel pressing against her heart. “What you need to be afraid of is – ”

But at that moment a roaring wind arose and wiped away the words.

She didn’t remember closing her eyes. It wasn’t as if she consciously fell asleep again. It was more like she slowly became aware of her body again, starting with her heart as it slowed back to normal, and her perception of it changed from a sound, to a pressure, and then a comforting rhythm. She awoke a few moments later, or at least it seemed like a few moments when it was more like a few hours. This time when her eyes opened there was canvas blocking her view. She climbed out from beneath her blankets and decided, since she couldn’t sleep, she might as well boil coffee and get serious about staying awake. Outside, in the fresh, moist air, heavy with the scent of pine and moss, she found a little old man sitting in a lotus position by the dying embers of her fire.

“What are you doing?” was all she could think to say.

“It’s something I saw on PBS,” he

told her. Painfully, he unraveled his legs. “I’m not sure about it, though. Hurts like hell.”

“You’re supposed to reach nirvana,” Angeline told him, recognizing the configuration from a yoga class she started but never finished. She stirred the fires dying embers, threw on another log or two, and sat down across from him. When she looked up, he was still there, giving her confidence that he was real. He was a small, brown and ancient man, wrapped in an Indian blanket that didn’t look like it had come from any tourist trap she’d ever worked in. The quality of the handicraft was too good.

He looked vaguely familiar. His hair was long and white. His smile was mischievous. The wrinkles on his face had been trained by that smile, flowing upward, and there were a lot of wrinkles. He seemed safe enough, so she let him stay.

“I’ve been waiting for you,” he told her. “What took you so long?”

Thinking he meant, *where had she been tonight?* she said, “I had to work.”

"For almost thirty years?"

She looked at him closely. There was a familiarity, like a nursery rhyme from childhood, or the Muzak version of a Lennon-McCartney song.

"Do I know you?" she finally asked.

"I know you better than you know me. But no matter," he said, rewrapping the blanket tightly around his shoulders. "What we don't know we find out soon enough."

She stared deeply into his eyes, but just couldn't place him. He was like her mother's heartbeat, just an echo in the distance she couldn't match to a face.

"There's work to do, of course, and it's time we get started," he told her.

"What kind of work?" she asked.

"Make repercussions. Ravel mysteries. Build myths and legends. These things don't happen on their own, you know. Some people keep things in balance. Some people take care of repercussions. That's my job. It's time you started learning it, too. Start small and build it big. Think diversion. That's what we need now."

As if she needed more complications in her life, she thought. Still, it was a talent she possessed. Repercussions were drawn to her naturally like disassociated spirits to water.

"How do I do that?" she asked.

"You can begin by paying your respects to your ancestors," he said.

"Where do I go – " But when she looked up, he was gone. She was more surprised by his sudden exit than she had been by the bear's abrupt appearance, just when she was beginning to trust her perception of reality.

Chapter Five

I. Paying Respects

Angeline didn't remember much about the Catholic orphanage where she had spent her precious, early bonding stage. She didn't and, yet, she did. It didn't stay with her in a series of visual images. If her first months of life were a restaurant, and decorating the walls was the only path to salvation, then she was lost. Instead, her early impressions clung to her the same way free association, coinciding with a trauma, can stick you with an obsession.

She did have a sensation, strong and involuntary. Drive-bys in the old neighborhood automatically drew a sinking feeling from the pit of her stomach. It was no different to her than dreams of floodwaters engulfing her.

Her first family was a collection of institutional smells, sympathetic but solicitous voices, the cold comfort of breasts without function or form, and lengthy periods of vast isolation.

She had a real mother, of course.

From what little she'd been able to learn through the Freedom of Information Act, the woman had been a drifter, a carnival worker whose migratory range had covered most of the Upper Midwest. She'd interrupted her travels long enough to bring Angeline into the world and place her in an orphanage. Her mother had been decidedly blond, and suspiciously alcoholic, Angeline had discovered in the scant orphanage records. Talk about discouraging, though orphanages were known for exaggerating such shortcomings. It was considered merciful, to discourage future efforts to find birth mothers.

The official line went something like this; it was better for the children to forget the past and move on.

For Angeline, moving on had meant adoption. Even that hadn't exactly been the fulfillment of Little Orphan Annie's most secret hopes.

Her adoptive parents were already in their early forties when the orphanage called. At forty years old, it wasn't easy to adopt. "Would you be interested in a difficult child to place — a club foot or an Indian girl?" That's how the orphanage administrator had posed the question. Apparently someone else had grabbed the club-footed baby before Angeline's parents could decide.

Her adoptive parents had done the best they could raising her – for northern Europeans. But, for some reason, Angeline had never really bonded with her mother. Maybe it was the expectations — a baby girl to complete the picture, to add the missing piece to her parents' unfulfilled marriage. But there was more than a child missing from that marriage.

In fact, adopting a child made the problems more apparent, instead of solving them. With Angeline in the house there were no more excuses. Well, there was one more. They adopted a blond-haired boy two years later and that hadn't solved anything either.

It wasn't as if she blamed her parents, much. Everyone had their own baggage to carry. Her parents were no exception. Neither was Angeline, for that matter. But Angeline's fatal flaw, in the classic Greek literary sense, had nothing to do with her parents. Her parents were almost moot, except for the Catholic guilt-complex they'd imposed on her at an early age. No matter. She'd shed that quickly and easily. She'd always had a talent for cutting to the chase. It was nice Jesus had died for her parents' guilt but that had nothing to do with her.

She had bears to deal with.

II. Island Art

By Tuesday, the TV cameras still hadn't arrived, but irony had: "Weekly Croquet Tournament, Made Possible by Your White Ancestors. Stake-Driving Begins Every Saturday at noon."

On the Island, sarcasm was an art form.

The crowd at the cemetery had disappeared, apparently having grown tired of the subject already, dispersing to favorite nooks for coffee and gossip about who was sleeping with whom. The ribbon of yellow tape that demarked the cemetery grounds was the most colorful change. A single sentinel sat in a lawn chair near the cemetery entrance, a young man with shoulder-length black hair and a scowl.

Most eyes would have seen the scowl and been discouraged. Angeline's eyes saw someone who'd been on a lonely vigil for more than a day now and was probably starving for conversation.

"Have the tour buses started lining up for the show?" she asked.

His head snapped back like someone struck between the eyes by a mixed message.

"Oh, I know what it is. I look Native American but I've got a urban attitude. It throws a lot of people off," she explained.

"I should know better," he answered. "I grew up in the city, adopted out when I was a baby. My whole family was broken up and sent to homes all over the Midwest."

His name was Jay. He was younger than Angeline. He wore rings on his fingers and she felt comfortable with that common trait. When he was a baby, the welfare department had removed him, his brother and five sisters from their home on Madeline Island, scattering them to the winds. He landed in Beloit, Wisconsin, on the Illinois border. Beloit was a little city with big-city problems — racial tension and gangs to fill the void left by broken families. When he was growing up, he didn't know he had blood parents, brothers and sisters, aunts and uncles. One by one, over the years, the children had wandered home. Jay, the youngest, was the last to return. By the time he washed up on the Island shore, both his parents had died.

The tribal elders had asked him to watch the cemetery. The tribal elders were like that. Find a young man with a passion for his heritage and put him to work right away, give him a role, a place in the community.

"The elders got me hanging here so there's no more trespassers until this thing is settled," he told her.

Settled meant deciding once and for all where the boundary was and erecting a fence to define it.

"Where's Madeline's grave? Is it marked?"

"You want to see it?"

She did. There was a stone marker, tilted backward by nearly a hundred and fifty years of winter's frozen contractions and spring's upheavals. It wasn't much different from many of the markers in the cemetery. "Neglected" wasn't the right word. More like, "tended as well as possible by those caught in the grip of survival with little time or few resources, even for their ancestors." There were coins stacked on top of the marker.

"It's kind of a tradition. They leave coins for the dead, in case they need anything," he explained.

"Do you need anything?" she asked as they turned back toward the gate.

"Hot coffee is good any time," he

told her.

"I'll bring some next time I come," she promised.

His eyes narrowed as he looked at her intently.

"Are you really Anishinabe?" he asked.

Angeline looked up suddenly, caught by surprise.

"I'm sorry. I haven't heard that word in a long time. I can't even remember where it was. But truthfully, I don't know what I am. I mean, at the orphanage they said I was Indian, but there's no real proof — no paper trail."

"I know a way," he said, stepping closer "Tell me what you see when I say ... uh, migizi."

"Hm. An eagle?"

He couldn't hide the surprised look on his face.

"Waawaashkeshi ..."

"Deer?"

"Makwa ..."

"That one I already knew. It means 'bear.' She turned and left him to his confusion, Angeline recalling a talent she'd had for reading road signs. She looked back once while she was walking away.

He looked lonely sitting in his chair trying to maintain a stern look on his face. It struck her she was seeing an anomaly. No Ojibwe lived on the Island anymore. There were, in fact, many more Ojibwe gravesites than homes containing living members of the tribe that once called Madeline Island its spiritual center.

III. Chaos Happens

Someone with great insight decided, at a time now forgotten, in a way never fully understood, to build a gazebo near the entrance to the ferry boat dock. Angeline and Equilibrium were both grateful as they sat beneath the structure sharing a lunch of tuna sandwiches from a Styrofoam box.

"Sometimes I think you're the only person who has it all figured out," Angeline told her friend. She swallowed, then added, "and sometimes I think you're totally crazy."

"Mm. Me, too," Equilibrium answered through a mouthful of tuna and enriched bread.

"I have this bumper sticker on my Suzuki. It says, 'Chaos happens.' That's the sum and total of my philosophy on life. I try not to get too philosophical. How's the sandwich?"

"Mm!" Equilibrium tried to answer.

"My philosophy is that it all looks like chaos. There doesn't seem to be a reason for any of it. But if people could see what I can see ... and it's not like I ever really wanted to see all these spirits and things ... But if people could see it all, it would make more sense." She lifted the sandwich to her mouth for a bite, but thought of something else to say first. "It's like those Greek tragedies, or comedies, or whatever, where gods that are more human than humans, and are jerking all our chains, rattling everyone's cages, just because immortality has long stretches of extreme boredom."

Angeline watched as a truck with a satellite dish perched on top and the words "Channel 3 News" written on the side, drove off the ferry, up the dock and past the two women.

"Mm?"

"Maybe you're right," Angeline decided. "Maybe it still wouldn't make any sense."

IV. Perception Becomes Reality

The TV cameras arrived on Wednesday.

The on-the-scene TV personality interviewed Tom's cousin, the Town Chairman, who was still dressed in the work clothes he always wore when inspecting highway construction. There wasn't any highway construction on the Island that day, but he was on the county board, too, and the county was always building a road to somewhere. Besides, the grey cotton work clothes went well with his 1970s sideburns and mustache. He looked uncomfortable in front of the camera but tried to say all the right things.

"We've always gotten along with the Chippewas. This was an unfortunate incident, but I'm sure we'll set it right. I know Rev. Olson personally and he wouldn't do anything on purpose to insult the Chippewas."

They interviewed the Rev. Olson who frantically explained it was all a dreadful mistake. He just didn't know where the boundary was. But this was probably the best thing that could have happened, he said, adding that he knew he took his croquet too seriously and this was just the humbling experience he needed.

The Tribal spokesperson was a political activist and U.S. Army vet named Norm. Norm attended the film session wearing his old army fatigue jacket and the scars from various political battles over the years. He said the tribe was awaiting a decision by the district attorney to see if he planned to prosecute the Rev. Olson for trespassing. Until then, they were simply trying to prevent the whole thing from being blown out of proportion. Although the tribe had other important priorities to consider, tribal members were understandably upset.

"We're certain the Rev. Olson wasn't intentionally trying to insult the Ojibwe people. But that's just the point," he said in a voice that indicated he'd been in front of a TV camera before. "It's not unusual for the white community to offend the Ojibwe community without trying."

Then, since they were there, the TV camera crew interviewed the Island tourism director and collected happy-face, file footage for use at a later time.

They also interviewed Tom.

"I'm not surprised this happened. It's happened before — when the lagoon was dredged in the 1960s, when the sewer project was built about fifteen years ago. Ojibwe remains have been unearthed with complete disregard over and over during the past three hundred years and nothing's changed. It's not just the bones, or the burial mounds, or the Spirit Stone or the Island. You can't treat a peoples' beliefs with respect until you learn to treat the people with respect."

His comments didn't make the final edit.

Then everyone went to the museum for a tour where they ran into Ben, who was standing pensively staring at a large stone on the ground. He invited the crew and spokespeople to his walk-in hell for coffee and conversation. On entering The Restaurant, the "on-air personality" was lost for words momentarily to describe her first impressions of his eating establishment. She finally came up with "unique" delivered with a forced smile. He took it as a compliment. Then he slipped into talking about Chicago in the sixties, the camera crew reminded the on-the-scene personality they had a deadline.

V. Missing Footage

Back at the TV studio in Duluth the deadline became real for the on-the-scene-live-TV-personality. With minutes to go and counting before the perception became reality, the on-the-scene-live-TV-personality raced through the studio hallway carrying carefully crafted news copy for the on-the-air-live-personality to read. The less-than-live-TV-executive stopped her for a behind-the-scenes update.

"How did it go out on the Island," he asked his TV-personality.

"We got some good actualities and the story has potential. It could heat up," his TV-personality responded.

Down the hall, the cameraman popped his head out the door of the editing room, and motioned for the TV-personality. She saw his frantic motions, excused herself and went to the editing room.

"What's up?" she asked as she entered the room.

"Tell me I'm not losing my mind," the cameraman said, seeking reassurance.

"You're not losing your mind. Why? What happened?"

"Look at this."

He pushed a button and videotape played out on the monitor in front of him. The video displayed a grassy lawn at the museum and, in the center of the frame, a square of grass that hadn't seen sunlight in weeks.

"What happened to the big stone?" the TV-personality asked.

"You saw it, too, didn't you? I'm not the only one? But somewhere between here and there it disappeared," the cameraman said.

"If it was ever really there," the TV-personality said.

The two media professionals exchanged wary, telling looks.

"I won't say anything about this if you won't," the TV-personality offered.

"Works for me."

VI. Polarity

Once the news segment aired, polarity set in. Nearly everyone felt obligated to choose sides. It was an Island trait. More than three centuries of association with the Ojibwe Tribe hadn't softened the obsession. It didn't matter if the conflict involved treaty rights, or whether Jamie was right in publicly chastising Hermiette at The Tavern after she encouraged the advances of some well-heeled Minneapolis tourist who, by the way, wasn't half-bad looking and it was empty flattery anyway and she knew it.

It didn't matter. There were sides to be taken and that's all that counted. There was a pattern to this choosing sides that normally went something like this:

A few of the opinion-shapers on either side of the issue staked out their positions early and often. People like Tom and his cousin Bernie were predictable that way. Bernie usually waited to see what Tom was going to do and then did the opposite.

Others waited to see what Ted and Charley had to say about it before making up their minds. There were economic interests in play.

Ted and Charley owned the two largest taverns on the Island. Like almost everything else in this closed culture, their contrasting personalities helped maintain a social balance. Ted had the more successful of the two drinking establishments located near the marina, a tavern heavy with tradition and a décor that never changed. He regarded the croquet incident as a "tempest in a teapot." Charley's business was on the other end of the Island near the ferry dock. He moved the furniture around weekly and changed the menu almost as often. Charley was sympathetic with the outraged. People's drinking habits changed accordingly.

Once the major players were on record, the conflict made its way into one-liners, heated political debate and pick-up lines. On the Island, any reason to get laid was a good reason.

Jamie and Hermiette were seen at The Tavern arguing about political correctness. She was "for." He was "against". They began socializing at separate saloons.

Word of the croquet incident spread. Bus tours arrived from Minneapolis, bringing senior citizens who were promised a package deal that included stops at both local casinos and the Indian Cemetery. They piled out of the buses wearing flowered Hawaiian shirts, taking pictures with pre-programmed, thirty-five millimeter cameras they didn't know how to operate. Jay started wearing mirrored sunglasses to protect his eyes from the telescoping flashes popping in his face in broad daylight. He was developing a flashbulb-reflex, she noticed when she brought him a cup of hot coffee in the early evening before returning to her camp. She genuinely felt sorry for him, but didn't stay. She knew a gathering flood when she saw one. She planned a relaxed night at home by the campfire.

She was grateful she didn't have a TV set. She preferred good conversation with friends and wandering spirits.

This night she didn't actually have to fall asleep before the little old man showed up in her camp. All she had to do was put the coffee on and turn her back to light her smudge pots.

"If you're going to keep coming back every time I make coffee you should probably tell me your name. Otherwise, I won't know what to call you," she told him.

"Call me Grandfather," he answered.

"I could use a grandfather about now," she said, sitting across the fire from him, wrapping herself in her own blanket — a quilt stitched by little old Norwegian women in a church basement.

"Things are going well, don't you think? Well, of course, you wouldn't know. You don't know what we're trying to do yet," he told her, smiling.

"I was going to say something

about that. You want to let me in on things?"

"It doesn't work that way. You have to discover the answers as we go along," he said, holding his cup of coffee in both hands, breathing in the aroma, or at least the steam she could see rising from his cup.

"Why? Is that some kind of a tradition or something?"

"You learn better that way. You learn and then you think, 'Ah, I was so clever to figure that out,' and then you'll never forget it."

"I should have known it would be hard," she responded, breathing deeply from her own coffee cup.

Neither of them spoke for several minutes. She didn't know what his excuse was, but she was trying to figure out just what it was she was supposed to figure out. She had gone to the cemetery. She'd done the ancestor thing. Even if she wasn't entirely sure who her ancestors were, the Ojibwes were here and here was home. They called themselves “Anishinabe,” or “original people,” so it all traced back to them anyway.

Other than that, no one except Tom and, maybe the crazy girl she’d fed leftovers to a few nights before, had offered anything resembling a reasonable theory. Maybe Equilibrium was right. Maybe this was all a matter of balance.

“Have you met the crazy blond? From Minneapolis?”

“Who?”

“She said her name’s Equilibrium. She’s always offering hand jobs?”

“So, she calls herself Equilibrium these days. I’ve known her for a while. We’ve worked together before, and she’s not as crazy as she sounds. Humans always think that about those who can walk in and out of the spirit world at will. You should know something about that.” He looked up at her over the top of his coffee cup with a glance that said they were members of the same exclusive club, one defined by unfavorable public opinion the same way the Inquisition defined the real intellectuals of its time and had brought them all together in the same cell blocks. "The rules in the spirit world are different than this physical world. When you travel back and forth from one to the other you can get as confused as a commuter flying from coast to coast."

"One thing's for certain, this whole incident thing is growing faster than teen pregnancy," she said, as much to herself as to her guest. There was something in his sly smile that confirmed her suspicions.

"Give me a hint," she implored.

"You should know. Something was lost and now he wants to come home," the old man answered.

"Just like me."

"Just like you."

"How?"

He frowned, as if growing impatient with a child.

"You remember I said something

about a diversion?"

"A diversion?" She vaguely recalled that he had mentioned it last time, but —

"Don't think too hard on it. You'll hurt yourself," he chastised her. "I tried already, learned something about croquet, too. I could be good at that. But it wasn't big enough. We need bigger."

"How?"

"You start small. I'll make it big. Don't worry. You'll know what to do. You can't help it. That's why you're here, because I need your help. No other reason."

"And here I thought it was to find my roots."

"There's time for that, too. I'll send someone to help. But right now we need a diversion. You'll know what to do. You can't help it."

VII. Rearranging the Furniture

Things were getting really bad and were threatening to spill off the Island.

Equilibrium understood that better than anyone. She was running out of options.

There was one technique she hadn't tried yet, but there was a problem. Standing in the shadows behind a tree near the Indian Cemetery, even she understood the obstacle in her way.

She'd liked it better when everyone had neglected the cemetery. That way, when she needed to change the balance of things, no one noticed her. She could slip in and rearrange the coins on the headstones without being seen. Not everyone knew about the coins. People came to visit the graves and they left coins behind. She thought maybe they figured the coins would come in handy wherever the spirits were. She didn't know. Sometimes when there got to be too many coins, and the Island was losing its balance, she'd take some of them. She wasn't stealing. She was balancing.

But now there was a man in the way, guarding it so she couldn't just go into the cemetery and balance things. Luckily, there wasn't any moon. She noticed things like that. Most people only saw the moon when it was full and romantic. She felt it when it was gone. That was her time to take action. She saw the man's head nod and then his chin fell onto his chest. She waited until she heard him breathing deeply, and then made her move.

VIII. Breakfast in Hell

That whole thing about not being able to help it bothered Angeline. What was that, anyway? Was she so predictable, or worse yet, compulsive, obsessive, she thought as she beat the life out of pancake batter in the kitchen at the local walk-in hell.

It was still early with no customers yet. Those who had gone to bed at a reasonable hour — reasonable for the Island — weren't awake yet, and those who had stayed up all night had skipped past hunger all the way to whatever itches they could never scratch enough. Good thing, too. She was in a bad mood and beating batter and cutting things with a sharp knife helped to get it out of her system.

"I don't know what he expects from me," she muttered to herself, referring to Grandfather.

"'You'll know when the time comes,'" she mimicked him. "'You won't be able to help yourself,' like I'm some kind of obsessive-compulsive."

For a spirit, he was acting so human, she thought. It was like she was some kind of chess piece and he was the only one playing the —

There was a knock on the back door. She knew that knock, like someone apologizing for taking up space in your universe.

She greeted Equilibrium, offered her coffee, but understood when the girl said all she really needed was plain old water. Angeline apologized for being busy, but listened while she worked,

"I was so worried," the girl explained, her expression underscoring her message. "About the big imbalance and all, but I think I took care of it."

"I don't know what we'd do without you," Angeline said, only half-listening as she mixed a bowl of scrambled eggs.

"I can feel it, it's all better now. I've always been sensitive that way."

"It's a hard job, but somebody has to do it," Angeline intoned.

"I'm hungry now. I think I can eat without upsetting the balance. I even have money, see?" She held out a collection of coins in her hand.

Angeline looked up from her work. She hated to think how Equilibrium earned her cash.

"That's OK. My treat."

"No, I can pay."

"Really, you don't – "

But Equilibrium rushed up to Angeline, took her hand, and poured the coins into it. Angeline stared at the coins, then straight into Equilibrium's eyes.

"How did you get this money?"

Angeline felt compelled to ask, still holding the coins in her cupped hand, unable to put them in her pocket just yet.

"Promise not to tell?" Equilibrium asked, looking down at her feet. Now Angeline was really worried.

"Where?" She was aware her voice sounded alarmed. That was her intention. "Where?"

"The cemetery."

"Not from the graves!"

"Yes," she confessed.

"We have to put them back, right away!"

Angeline asked the other waitress to cover for her and promised she'd be back before it got busy. As she left, she poured a large cup of coffee to go.

"Here's the plan," she told Equilibrium as they approached the cemetery. "I'll distract Jay and you put the coins back. You remember what graves you took them from, don't you?"

"Mostly."

"Do the best you can."

Jay was reading a newspaper as Angeline approached, offering him the cup of coffee, "just like I promised."

"You're an angel." He accepted the cup, sipped it first, and then drank deeply, issuing a satisfying sigh when he was done. Behind him, Angeline saw Equilibrium creeping into the cemetery.

"Anything good in the paper?" Angeline asked.

"Something about those copper mines in Upper Michigan ... They want to dump acid in the mines, float the copper to the surface. Some kind of new mining process."

"I don't like the sound of that." She watched as Equilibrium carefully balanced a stack of coins on a gravestone.

"Worst part is, they want to ship the acid by train, over the Rez'. What happens if the train derails? Bye-bye Rez'."

"Somebody ought to do

something." A gust of wind caught the newspaper, but Jay gathered the pages together before the wind could carry them to a higher level in the atmosphere.

"What can you do? Big business ... They can buy and sell you and me."

"There's ways," Angeline said. "Like a demonstration, or a blockade, or something."

"That stuff doesn't work anymore. Nobody listens," Jay scoffed.

"You have to try! And what do you mean nobody listens. How many reporters have been out here this week? And this is small!" The force of her conviction left Jay, momentarily, with nothing to say. The wind struck again, this time carrying the front page, the classifieds and the daily-horoscope away. When Jay had to choose between the paper and his steaming cup of coffee, and he chose to save the coffee.

"What was that?"

"Me, I think. It's been happening when I get pissed."

“Don’t ever get pissed at me,” he implored.

He didn’t know, couldn’t know that her imperative tone was induced by the stress of the moment. Angeline glanced back and saw Equilibrium balance another set of coins on a second headstone, and then slip out of the cemetery.

“You really think it could work?”

“I don’t know, but you have to try,” she answered, relaxing with each step Equilibrium put between herself and the cemetery.

IX. A Short Free Tour

The call had come from out of nowhere. Because of that Hutch and Brewster found themselves walking down a railroad line toward the railroad bridge on the Bad River, following an old man in bib overhauls – a white man at that.

He was a grizzled old man, deep into his seventies. His face and hands showed the wear and tear that comes from a lifetime spent doing manual labor outdoors, at the mercy of the elements. His face was tanned and leathered. The knuckles on his hands knobby and swollen, his fingers bent at unnatural angles.

He led the way, the contingent from the tribe following.

"The last train that went through here was traveling 15 miles an hour and everyone held their breaths the whole way," he said. He spoke the truth like someone sick and tired of nice lies and the people who said them. He spoke the truth like someone used to dealing directly with a hard life. He spoke the truth like someone on a railroad pension — he could tell the whole world to take a flying leap. He'd paid his dues and could do what he wanted now.

"The ties are rotted and the gravel bed might as well not even be here." He stopped and kneeled down. "But here's your real problem." He reached out to a railroad spike and, with his bare hand, pulled it out. "That's supposed to keep the rail upright. Without it, the only thing holding the rail in place is the weight of the train."

X. Un-Equilibrium

Equilibrium thought it was kind of fun working on a plan with Angeline. Not many people had ever wanted to help Equilibrium maintain the balance before and, besides that, Angeline was good at creating diversions.

"I'd have never thought of coffee," Equlibrium told herself.

She remembered which graves she'd taken the coins from, but not exactly. She tried to put them back the way she'd found them and knew it was only close. She slipped out of the cemetery and met Angeline on the return route to The Restaurant.

"You did the right thing," Angeline told her as they quickly walked along the road. "Now it's all fixed."

Equilibrium didn't want to contradict Angeline, because her friend had a good soul, probably an old soul, too, and Angeline thought she was doing the right thing. But in her heart, Equilibrium knew this meant imbalance, and that meant trouble.

Equilibrium excused herself and headed to the north end of the Island and a good place to hide, at least for a few days.

XI. The Glass House

The Glass House in Toronto rose above the skyline as a testament to mining men and their kind. Like most glass houses built in major urban centers, those residing inside had a fine view of the world, as they knew it. Those at street level, however, could catch no glimpse of the inner workings, no hints of the weighty decisions, and no share in the wealth.

In a corner office on an upper floor, two men stood near the floor-to ceiling windows looking out on the world at their feet.

"It's beautifully simple," the idea man, a vice-president-of-something-or-other, told the CEO. "We pour millions of gallons of water down the old mine shafts, water laced with sulfide. The sulfide loosens the remaining copper ore and floats it to the surface where we scoop it up. We cap the mineshafts and leave the sulfide there for eternity, or the corporate equivalent of eternity. We can get all the water we need from Lake Superior and ship all the sulfide we need with the railroad. It's like playing with your toys in the bath tub."

"Do you expect any opposition?" the CEO asked.

"Nothing organized."

The CEO continued to look out pensively through the glazed glass.

"Nice view," the idea man commented. "You sometimes feel like a god way up here?"

The CEO turned and looked, smiled slightly, and looked back out the window.

"It's tempting at times. Very tempting."

XII. The Bigger Diversion

Hutch sat on the back porch of his simple family house on the reservation wrapping leather strands around a long wooden staff, binding eagle feathers to its top, listening to Jay go on and on about something.

"Think about it, man. Think about the Exxon Valdez. What happens if the train derails — bye, bye Rez'," Jay pleaded his case.

"It couldn't be you're just looking for a way off cemetery guard duty, could it?" Hutch asked. "Besides, the tribal council is taking care of it."

"OK, I admit it. It's mostly boring out there on the Island and when it isn't it still sucks. But that's not the thing. Being right is the thing."

"Being right doesn't mean squat. Being bigger and badder means everything. Besides, nobody pays any attention to protests anymore." He focused on the task at hand. There was something about keeping his hands busy that made him think clearly.

"You couldn't be more wrong. Check out the cemetery. How many TV cameras have been there? And that's small. This is big."

Hutch looked up from his work and looked at Jay, staring intently as if looking for answers in Jay's face — his eyes alive with passion for what he was saying. There had been a time, Hutch remembered, when he had that kind of enthusiasm. Where had it gone? It wasn't like a thief snuck in one night and took it all. It was more like small pieces taken out of him every time he stopped long enough in one place for his fate to catch up with him. There was the time he saw his parents for the first time, really saw them, saw how tired they were, how human they were, how worn out they were.

But here was Jay, his face flush with passion, his jaw set, barely able to contain this call to action. Hutch stood stiffly, gripping the lance firmly, testing its balance. Suddenly, it all felt right. With that feeling, he didn't need any other confirmation.

"Then let's go do this thing."

XIII. The Blockade

The thin, silver rails sliced through the reservation like the conservative evangelical wing of the Republican Party marching to defend America from the National Endowment for the Arts – with impunity and a complete disregard for any collateral damage.

The sun was just beginning to rise, painting a bright red sky behind it.

From the nearby tree line, Hutch walked out into the open space, Brewster covering his back, Jay hanging back. Hutch stopped, handed the lance to Brewster, and scanned the nearby trees. He saw one he liked, a strong one that had apparently weathered a few storms and he walked directly to it. He walked behind and, slightly screened by it, removed his tobacco pouch. He said a prayer and put down tobacco in the six directions.

When he was ready and walked

back to his brother, retrieved the lance and the group walked to the nearby railroad grade. He stepped over the rails, walking along the gravel grade a few paces before stopping. Leaning the lance in the crook of his arm, Norm opened a small leather pouch, removed tobacco, and spread it on a small portion of the railroad grade. Then, he lifted the lance high above him, and drove it downward into the gravel between the steel rails. Looking upward, he saw a bird flying at high altitude above them. The bird, a mature bald eagle, descended and landed in a nearby tree.

"This is the right thing to do," Hutch said, more to himself than Jay. "I only hope its a good thing, too."

XIV. Spillage

The Ashland County District Attorney sat alone at his desk in his Ashland County Courthouse office. Because of boundaries that could only have been drawn by a drunken state government official in the 19th century, Madeline Island was located in Ashland

County. The county seat was in Ashland, at the bottom of Chequamegon Bay, twenty miles and a ferry ride from the Island.

That put the DA right in the middle of the croquet incident. Now he had to decide whether a Methodist minister had been trespassing when a game of croquet spread onto Ojibwe, formerly Catholic and, before that Qjibwe, burial grounds.

The phone rang. He glanced at the clock on the wall, the kind of plain, round clock with large black numbers you can only find in government offices or public schools. He was late for Friday night dinner with his mother. It was a weekly ritual. Every Friday he, his wife and their kids, joined his mother for fish dinner. They usually went to a fish boil, if they could find one, and in northern Wisconsin you could find one almost every weekend. A fish boil was the region's non-meat equivalent of Mulligan stew. Recipes were carefully guarded secrets handed down from father to son through the generations.

The ringing phone demanded immediate attention. He picked up the receiver.

"Ashland County District Attorney's Office."

It was the sheriff.

"There's going to be trouble," the sheriff said over the phone. A group on the Bad River Reservation was blocking the train tracks, refusing to allow a load of sulfide through to the White Pines Copper Mine in the Upper Peninsula. The sheriff wanted a ruling on the legal options.

The district attorney promised he would look into it and get back to him. The DA hung up the phone, folded his hands under his chin and thought for a moment.

This might be just what he was looking for. Maybe the whole train episode would get big enough to divert everyone's attention. Then he could decide on the trespassing charge involving that Madeline Island thing without anyone noticing. He could pass off any decisions about the train to the state, or better yet, the feds. He felt a little lighter as he turned off the lights, left the office and locked the door.

XV. The Sheriff

The Ashland County Sheriff put the phone receiver back in its cradle and sighed heavily. He hated Indian trouble.

He was a sheriff and he liked the world black and white – good guys and bad guys and laws that are hard and fast. But with Indian trouble, there were just a lot of grey areas and who knew what the laws really said, not since the federal courts got involved.

The federal courts had gotten involved back in the 1970s and 1980s with treaty rights and decided that the tribes could gather resources in the whole northern third of Wisconsin, what they called the ceded territory, even on public lakes and private land. What a mess that had been, he thought to himself. The white population – well, at least the angry ones — didn't take to the idea and had staged violent protests at the boat landings.

This sheriff was undersheriff at the time. The sheriff, his boss, was an egomaniac and power monger. It was the sheriff who had told his understudy, “County sheriff is the most powerful job in the State of Wisconsin … in any state for that matter. They can tell you what to do but nobody can make you do it.”

During treaty rights, the state had insisted on more county protection at the boat landings to protect the tribal fishermen from the protesters. The old sheriff had insisted on state money to pay the cost. He ended up giving only as much protection as the state paid for.

In a way, that’s how the new sheriff got his job. The state swooped in with an army of investigators who didn’t stop nosing around until they had something on the old man. They got him for helping himself to choice guns from the evidence locker. The investigators found automatic rifles in his private collection. Gave one to his son. Stupid, really, but the real stupidity was in thinking he could do anything he wanted while thumbing his nose at the state attorney general.

The sheriff looked around the office. He heard, down the hall in the antiquated jail cells, the echo of someone's misery. It was time to go home. He needed a drink. He was planning on cutting back, maybe quitting altogether, but tonight he needed a drink real bad. He hoped there wouldn't be Indian trouble. Most of all, he hoped he wouldn't be forced to do something he really didn't want to do.

Chapter Six

I. Sulfuric Acid

When the Europeans first arrived on Lake Superior's shores in the seventeenth century, the copper was so thick in Michigan's Gogebic Range that white men, to the dismay of the Ojibwe, could pick up and carry off huge nuggets found resting on the surface.

However, the Ojibwe reacted to most acts of pilfering by Europeans with horror and offered multiple gifts to the spirits to atone for any such losses, apologizing for the barbarians.

For most of the late nineteenth century and much of the early twentieth, the Gogebic Range provided 70 percent of the nation's copper supply. Then it played out.

The mines staggered on, using more refined mining techniques, until if appeared that the last of the underground copper mines would be closed.

Then came sulfide mining. Sulfide mining ... it had to be the brainchild of a megalomaniac fed a steady dose of Tinker Toys, Lincoln Logs, and erector sets in childhood. In that world a deep shaft mine becomes an anthill with Lake Superior the place to attach the garden hose.

Sulfide compounds would be shipped over railroad lines into the Upper Peninsula. The sulfide would be mixed with water from Lake Superior and pumped into the old mine shafts to loosen the remaining copper. The copper would be extracted after it floated to the surface. The sulfuric acid, eleven billion gallons of it, one thousand times more toxic material than the Exxon Valdez spilled into Prince Edward Sound, would be left in the shafts — on purpose. According to the prevailing theory, the stone shafts would contain the acid, preventing it from migrating into Lake Superior.

A group of Ojibwe tribal members had a different theory.

In their worst-case scenario, the train would derail while traveling across the Bad River Reservation on tracks that hadn't been used to carry any substantial freight for decades. A derailment would mean destruction of the Bad River and the irreplaceable wild rice sloughs where the river emptied into Lake Superior. It could also mean wholesale death and disease. It had happened before on smaller scales. More than one truck and tanker filled with chemical waste had been seen with its engine idling on a back road, a hose leading into the water and the spigot left open.

Tribal members still talk about the paper mill landfill that leeched dioxin into the water supply near Old Odanah. Cancer deaths followed in surrounding households.

To counter the prospect of a trainload of sulfuric acid crossing the reservation, tribal members blocked the tracks to prevent the worst-case scenario.

They built a spiritual barrier across the tracks and held vigil in a nearby camp. They affixed eagle feathers on lances and placed the lances in the ground at each of the four directions. That meant two lances sunk into the railroad grade, between the steel rails, east and west. Nothing else barred the trains from passing.

II. Classified

"We should go to Bad River. Maybe we can give moral support to what they're doing?" Angeline suggested, toying with her breakfast at Tom's Burned Down Cafe. Angeline liked making moral decisions. She welcomed dilemmas the way most people welcomed guest spots on game shows. She was good at it. She couldn't help herself.

Her sense of morality had been honed by the orphanage during her early bonding months, her frequent contact with bears, and a general disgust for all things painful to the human heart, hers in particular.

"I went last night," Tom told her. Apparently he had a sense of morality that needed constant feeding, too. "If you can wait until I get this classified ad written, I might be free later."

"What classified?"

"I have to hire an archeologist, one who can mix drinks," he responded automatically, as if he hired archeologists with bartending experience all the time. It wasn't until he looked up from his work and noticed Angeline's puzzled expression that he thought to fill her in.

"My cousin decided I was right and the town board needs to protect Ojibwe burial sites. He claims an old book written by a complete fool fifty years ago proves there's burial sites on my property. He wants to condemn it for the public good."

"He's serious?"

"All the time. That's part of his problem. The rest is genetic."

"Where does the archeologist fit in?"

"I'll change the name of this place to 'Tom's Burned Down Cafe and Burial Grounds,' hire an archeologist-slash-bartender to cover my ass and have another good story to tell anybody who wants to listen."

"Are there really burial sites here?"

"Not likely, but who knows. You have to be careful just putting in a septic system on this Island."

He finished the ad and asked Angeline for her opinion. She regretted out loud not taking a few archeology classes when she had the chance.

"That's not the worst of it," he told her. "My cousin decided Madeline Island somehow wouldn't be complete without a miniature golf course. Can you imagine? A real golf course isn't bad enough."

"What are you going to do?"

"Hope it falls flat on its face. If not, invite the patron saint of irony to intervene."

Talk about a well-developed sense of morality, Angeline thought.

III. Taking Up a New Sport

Angeline made a point of walking past the construction site for the new miniature golf course on her way to work. Like a condominium complex along a secluded stretch of pristine beach, this structure was going up surprisingly fast. There had been a crude attempt to mimic the Island's legitimate institutions.

Golfers on the first hole had to putt the ball through a lighthouse that didn't look much like any lighthouse in the Apostle Island chain. Then, the serious golfer had to direct the ball onto the deck of a miniature ferry that carried it over a water hazard to a small Island that represented the green. For a real challenge, the sportsman could chip the ball into a lake trout's open mouth. Presumably the ball passed through the fish without causing internal damage and out a hole in the tail. On the ninth hole it was necessary to get the ball past a seagull swooping in to grab it, obviously mistaking it for junk food. No, wait. That was a real seagull.

But there was no walk-in hell, no burned-down cafes and no Indian Cemetery with its ancient markers, croquet hoops and tour buses.

Looking at it from the tourist's point of view, strictly for entertainment value, she could almost see the attraction. There was something in the human being which wants to feel like a giant Gulliver striding across a miniature world, fastidious about replacing divots, and careful not to step on the locals.

For her part, she wouldn't play until there was a blockaded railroad track. It just wouldn't be her perception of reality.

IV. Intent

It was a busy weekend at The Restaurant, which ended her hope of getting off early for a trip to the railroad protest camp. She had barely enough time to notice Saturday's front-page story about the blockade and a brief story on the back page about the district attorney's decision to not prosecute the

Rev. Olson. She wasn't sure how, but suspected the two had to be connected.

According to the DA, it was a matter of intent. The Rev. Olson hadn't intended any harm so apparently there wasn't any.

"Sure. It would have to be based on intent. Richard Nixon intended peace with honor in Vietnam and Charles Manson just intended to make a few new friends," Ben said with the kind of derisive overstatement he did so well.

Her mouth dropped open.

"What?" He used his impatient-with-the-world tone of voice.

"Sometimes, Ben, you truly amaze me," she told him, right before she kissed him on the cheek. He blushed.

"You could be good at that with practice," she told him.

V. On Meaningful Moments

The tour buses didn't run on Mondays, Jay told Angeline when she brought him a cup of coffee the next morning.

"I tried to get them to let me go down to the tracks, but they say I'm still needed here. Tell me what for. I don't see it," Jay complained.

A woman was standing vigil with him this time — an older woman whose dark hair was streaked with grey, but whose brown eyes were bright and alive. Her name was Orchid. She greeted Angeline with a nod, but didn't say anything for several moments as if studying her. Orchid stopped regularly at the cemetery to tend graves, she said. There were no Anishinabe living on the Island anymore, so she drove over on occasion from the Bad River Reservation.

"Some people think that because there are weeds in the cemetery that nobody cares," she told Angeline defensively. "But what looks better, a cemetery where the grass is clipped short like some skinhead's scalp, or this?"

This was more than just a dispute about bones, Orchid said. There were other things taken from the tribe over the years. There was the Big Drum, the tribe's ceremonial drum. It was in Florida now, in someone's private collection. "Like they can even use it ..."

Then there was the Spirit Stone. Although it was in the neighborhood, at the Madeline Island Museum, "That's not where he belongs." Orchid had dreams. The stone wasn't happy there, he told her. He wanted to return home.

"These things don't just happen. It's all connected. The tribe's medicine spirits are telling us something. It's time to come home," she said. The words struck Angeline in her heart, where human beings sometimes feel pain, and where she almost always did.

"Show her your 'Bone Donor Card,'" Jay prompted her.

"What's a Bone Donor Card?" Angeline asked.

"Show her," Jay urged again.

Orchid pulled a wallet from her bulky purse, removing a card and handing it to Angeline.

"'This card signifies that I am donating my bones to science,'" Angeline read aloud, "'if it means you'll stop digging up my ancestors.'"

Angeline asked for one of her own. Orchid had several. She placed one in Angeline's palm. Then she did something entirely unexpected.

"Do you have any tobacco?"

Angeline offered her a cigarette, but Orchid shook her head impatiently. Jay removed a pinch from a tobacco pouch and handed it to Orchid. She rubbed her forefinger in the tobacco and held it in the palm of her hand, looking into Angeline's eyes as she made small, circular motions. Then she reached up and touched Angeline, with that forefinger, on her heart. Her finger stayed there several moments, almost as if she was conducting the spiritual equivalent of a medical examination.

Then she withdrew her finger and announced that she had to run. Her mother was waiting in the car, "and she's not very good at it."

She didn't tell Angeline her diagnosis. Maybe because she sensed Angeline wasn't ready to know yet. There seemed to be more to Orchid than was apparent at first glance, Angeline thought. That fit her life these days.

It was a warm, sunny morning. The lake was bright blue and mirror-like. It was the first day during this summer when Angeline could feel the warm air driving the chill from her bones. It started at the outer edges, chipping away the permafrost which had formed the night before from sleeping on the ground, and all the way to Congress's attempt to kill off public broadcasting. That was cold. At this rate she'd be thawed before noon back to the time she handled her dad's funeral arrangements while her mother surrendered to denial.

Jay thanked her for the cup of hot coffee, but neglected it in deference to the sun's warm rays. He admitted it was an easy day as vigils went. Not that this vigil had been all that difficult. It was like life in many ways: long periods of boredom punctuated by sporadic flurries of intense activity, followed by rare meaningful moments.

The conversation had given Angeline a craving for a meaningful moment. She'd already had enough long periods of boredom in her life that she could draw on at will. It didn't look as if there would be sporadic periods of intense activity that morning, at least not here.

"Let's go work on the railroad," she suggested.

Jay knew exactly what she meant. Angeline drove while Jay smoked enough cigarettes for both of them. Angeline didn't even mind that he was smoking from her pack. As her Suzuki idled on the ferry dock, waiting for the next boat out, Angeline suddenly climbed out of the vehicle, leaving Jay to start a new cigarette, and walked to a nearby phone booth. She wasn't exactly sure where the inspiration had come from. Maybe it had something to do with meeting yet another mother figure in her life in Orchid.

Maybe she had suddenly regressed to some childhood age when she actually felt a bond with her mother, but she thought it was time to call home. Inside the phone booth, the old fashioned kind with a door and privacy, she felt herself actually looking forward to talking with her mother. She dialed the number, inserted a fistful of tips and waited.

"Hello?"

"Hi. I thought it was about time I called. How are you?"

"Hello? Who is this?"

VI. Working on the Railroad

It wasn't just the fact that her mother didn't recognize her voice, Angeline thought, although that hurt enough all by itself. It was the thought that her mother hadn't even expected a call, hadn't anticipated any kind of contact, and had probably written her daughter off altogether. And Angeline had been in such a good mood. That's the voice her mother didn't recognize. She probably would have known the defensive voice, or the sarcastic tone, what her mother called

Angeline's "attitude." Angeline had hung up the phone without another word and had vowed not to call again until she was feeling really pissy.

The Anishinabe Ogichidaa, "Original People Warriors," were between drum sessions when Angeline and Jay arrived beside the railroad tracks. They parked the Suzuki in a makeshift lot of other beat-up cars and trucks, an area beginning to resemble, from the disorder, a herd of milling ponies.

"Hey! They got tents. How come I don't get a tent?" Jay asked no one in particular, or the universe in particular.

"Think of your ancestors and the sacrifices they made," Angeline countered.

"Mine sacrificed me. Yours, too."

"At least yours didn't have a choice."

A camp had sprouted beside the tracks complete with a lodge built of bent tree branches. The lodge, with a tarp stretched over the top, served as kitchen and shelter from the occasional rain. Inside the shelter stood folding tables with small camp stoves, coolers of food and a few scattered cooking and eating utensils.

Lunch warmed on the stove.

Outside, a fire pit had been dug and ringed with stones, a small fire adding to ashes already accumulated in the pit. A few people were piling found-wood next to it. Folding chairs, a log and a couple of inviting stump ends surrounded the pit.

Someone greeted Jay. Someone else welcomed Angeline. Most importantly, a third person offered them both food.

They sat near the fire pit, Angeline choosing a stump end to sit on within view of the westernmost lance blocking the tracks.

"Ah-ho!" Norm greeted Jay. Norm, tall and thin with large square shoulders, was on the Bad River committee that oversaw negotiations with the district attorney.

"But I'm not here," he explained. "Officially, the Ogichidaa are on their own. That gives the council deniability talking with the railroad."

"How's everything at the cemetery?" Norm asked Jay.

"Quiet," Jay answered. "The food's better over there, though."

"You got that right. We sent someone out to find something, a rabbit, maybe. Anything for a change."

"Have any trains actually tried to get through?" Angeline asked between mouthfuls.

"No, we let them know right away what we were doing. That way, if they try getting through, we know they're running the blockade, not because of a scheduling error. But no, they haven't tried. I don't think they even trust these tracks. They used them a lot when the mines were busy, but they've been neglected for a good twenty years now."

"They should just pull them out and make a trail," Jay suggested.

“Snowmobile trail,” Norm added. “I’d get home a lot faster in the winter, I can tell you that.”

“The railroad never did anything for me,” Jay added.

“Funny thing, this is just about where the train would stop during my grandfather’s day to sell whiskey,” Norm said. He turned to Angeline to explain. “Back then, Indians couldn’t buy whiskey, so the train would stop here and unload at night, sell it right from the boxcar.”

The hunting party returned, consisting of two men wearing odd-lot camouflage clothing, one carrying a .22 caliber rifle which he leaned against the log by the fire pit so he could hold his paper plate of food.

“Anything?” Norm asked.

“Not a damn thing, except a bunch of bear tracks. Time to put out a spirit plate,” he suggested, before hungrily shoveling food into his mouth.

As they ate, a sheriff’s squad car

pulled up to the campground. The driver maneuvered, trying to find an obvious parking space among the haphazardly placed junkers as if he was lost without asphalt and neatly painted white lines.

"The man's here," one Ogichidaa intoned. No one turned to look.

The undersheriff walked toward them. He was the kind of person who considered himself an insider, able to talk with anyone about anything. To most tribal members, he was a vast improvement over past undersheriffs, but not exactly someone who walked and talked like an Ojibwe.

"Is he the one who just got out of treatment?" Jay asked.

"Naw, this is the one who just got divorced. I feel for the guy. He's not so bad," Norm said.

"I still don't like him. Call it my imprinting," Jay grumbled.

Still, they could joke with him about his college days in the 1960s when he wore his hair tied back in a ponytail, was resplendent in his tie-dyed T-shirts and beads, and smoked pot. Now he wore the brown sheriff's department uniform with all the whistles and bells. To tribal members, he did less harm than his predecessors and sometimes did some good. That was better than they were used to.

"Hear any news?" he asked as he pulled up a stump end near the fire pit.

"The hunting stinks," a man from the hunting party said, still eating.

The undersheriff glanced at the rifle.

"You know, it's probably not a good idea to have a weapon out in the open right now," he cautioned. "You've done a good job keeping this thing from escalating. I'd hate to see it get out of hand. Lord knows, you're the only ones who seem to know what you're doing with this."

"Sammy was just putting it back in his truck," Hutch explained. "Want something to eat?"

"Not this time. Apparently some railroad fat cats are on their way to town to start the talks. They can be more frustrating than the tribal council. I got to get back to town."

"You tell them everything's quiet out here. In fact, this might be the most boring place in the county right now," Hutch said, down on one knee, arranging fresh wood in the pit.

"Well, it looks like it's in the council's hands now," the undersheriff said.

"Could be," Hutch said, non-committally.

"I'll stop back later if I hear something," he said, and turned to leave. They watched him walk out of range.

"Nice guy, but not real savvy," the hunter said.

"Not much," Hutch agreed.

VII. America's Railroad

Railroad CEOs were like Major League baseball owners — adept at 19th century arrogance.

America needed the railroads, they insisted, just like they needed the New York Yankees and the Chicago Cubs. Railroads were more than a business. They were Americana. Toxic spill? That wasn't our derailment. That was America's derailment. PCBs near an abandoned roundhouse? That roundhouse isn't a Super Fund site. It's a historic landmark.

Paintings of great railroad men from the past still hung in the hallways at corporate headquarters across America, men like Cornelius and William Vanderbilt, James J. Hill, Collis P. Huntington, and J.P. Morgan, who sat for their portraits when the plains Indians were proudly riding horses and the birch bark canoe was the preferred form of transportation from one end of the bay to the other.

The relationship between Native Americans and railroads had always been strained.

To the Indians, railroads were a conflict with nature. They belched smoked; they made loud, shrieking sounds; they stopped for nothing, not animals, men on horses, or time. In the early days, they sent sparks flying that left forests and prairies smoldering ashes. The few 19th century Ojibwe who rode the railroads to Washington, D.C., to supplicate presidents for honest treaty enforcement, were left bone weary and disheartened by the experience. And always, the trains brought more white people who crowded the Indian territories.

A Wisconsin Central Railroad company car pulled into the parking lot at the new Chief Black Bird Tribal Administration Building in Odanah on the Bad River Reservation.

Several men in suits, carrying briefcases, stepped out of the car, but only after adjusting their power ties and smoothing their fresh haircuts. One man wore a wide-brimmed hat with a bird feather in the band and a vest with intricate beadwork. His name was Ryan Netherton, the chief negotiator. He hailed from the company's New Zealand branch where he'd cut his teeth negotiating with the Maori tribe. After stepping out of the car, the men paused before entering the building.

"Remember, we have to establish linkage. That's the key," Netherton said to the others with a decided New Zealand brand of British accent.

Inside the conference room tribal representatives, dressed somewhat less formally, waited for the railroad men.

"Remember, we can't let them establish linkage. That's the key," the tribal chairman reminded everyone, just before their guests entered the room. They shook hands with the railroad men. They offered coffee. They sympathized with the railroad men's plight. They understood the TV cameras had already been out to the site, and that could do no good for anyone.

Netherton accepted the coffee and handed out pouches of tobacco as gifts.

Of course, the tribal council could not speak for the Anishinabe Ogichidaa, but they knew their concerns. They worried about the condition of the tracks.

There had been the derailment in Duluth just two years earlier that spilled millions of gallons of benzene into the St. Louis River. Obviously, sulfuric acid held a greater potential for disaster than benzene. Basically, they told the railroad men, the Ogichidaa were concerned.

The tracks were safe, Netherton assured the tribal council. There were tracks in Ashland, just nine miles down the road, maintained on the same schedule as the line through the reservation, and that spur was still being used to haul coal from the dock on Chequamegon Bay.

The Anishinabe Ogichidaa were concerned about the railroad's ability to respond if there was a derailment and a spill.

The railroads had upgraded their response teams since the spill in Duluth, Netherton assured the council.

Then there was concern about whether the mineshafts would truly contain the sulfuric acid, or would it leech into Lake Superior. The Anishinabe were, after all, guardians of Kichi-gami.

Netherton was very sensitive to the Ojibwe's role in protecting the lake, he said. The process was safe, he assured.

The tribal council members said they felt quite assured, but of course, they couldn't speak for the Anishinabe Ogichidaa.

"Surely, as elders you must have some influence," Netherton insisted.

"Sadly, no," the tribal chairman said. "Being a tribal elder isn't what it used to be, not since before the railroads and the mines. My own son is out there and he's never listened to me."

The railroad men left without the linkage they so badly needed. Netherton and his entourage of men in suits and power ties filed from the room, assuring the tribal council they must all talk again soon.

Appearing defeated, the railroad men collectively looked like a man recently divorced out on his first dinner date in years, out of circulation far too long, who hadn't realized he had talked only about himself all night long. The truth didn't hit home until the dessert tray arrived.

Likewise, no one saw the small man who'd been sitting alone in a corner wrapped in a blanket, almost invisible to the corporate eye. He smiled to himself.

His people had learned much about negotiating since 1854, he told himself. The Ojibwe had learned to smile when they told negotiators to "go to hell." They'd learned deniability. They had learned they need not agree to anything when dealing from a position of strength. Most importantly, they were dealing from a position of strength and knew it.

He slipped out of the room quickly and quietly. He wanted to take a nap and then there was a PBS special about Eartha Kit he'd been looking forward to.

VIII. Magic

The fire blazed, the drums pounded, as the long northern summer evening slowly faded away. The summer solstice was barely a month past but it seemed to Angeline they would live forever tonight.

Her heart, the one which had caused her so much trouble most of her life, drew strength from the booming drums.

The crowd grew larger as the warm night air pulled its blanket over them, blocking out the sun. In the firelight, she caught glimpses of scenes as the light flickered about them, scenes that, like her dreams, seemed divorced from the strictures of time or the domineering advance of civilizations.

The fire flared and gave a view of a woman with a sleeping infant pressed against her breasts. The flames danced and illuminated the intense faces of men drenched in sweat, pounding on their drums, their expressions solemn and severe. Someone threw another log on the fire and a swarm of red sparks spiraled upward to join the stars. Just within the reach of the firelight, at the outer edges where light fought with the dark night for dominance. Angeline thought she saw others dancing, others drawn to the ancient and yet familiar sound of the drum as if it was a common call to the spirits of all worlds.

Diesel-driven trains pulling tankers of sulfuric acid would be party crashers here in more ways than one. Pistons driven up and down could not, and would not, attempt to match the beat of drums. Mechanization always demanded the human race follow its rhythm, a rhythm that normally grounded endeavors more human into dust. Certainly, diesel exhaust would conflict with the sweet smell of the surrounding forest and the fresh scent of the nearby river. Besides, the train had a different destination. The train had a schedule to keep with a profit-making venture. The camp, on the other hand, was the antithesis to schedules and profit-making ventures in general.

There was magic in the night, in the ways of the Anishinabek, and in the bond between these people and this earth. Not the kind of controlling magic Angeline's Western white background had taught her to pursue. This was not Superman's ability to leap tall buildings at a single bound. This wasn't Samantha's talents at twitching her pert nose and rescuing her hapless husband from socially awkward situations. It certainly wasn't virtual reality.

How could civilization do that to itself, Angeline wondered, how could it deliver itself to the doorstep of close-but-not-warm-and-soft, not even hot-and-hard? How could anything that wasn't wet, didn't smell of hormones and didn't bleed once a month ever become the objective just because it stimulated the senses and was compliant?

If this night was magic, it was the magic of knowing, understanding and, therefore, accepting.

"Don't these drums just make you want to jump up and boogie?" Jay asked, dropping onto the ground beside her.

"I don't dance," she answered as if it was some kind of moral commitment she'd made years earlier instead of a rationalization to cover her insecurities. "Hey! This is your chance." Jay leaped to his feet, grabbing her arm as if this was a freshman mixer and he was trying to draw her onto the dance floor. "C'me on, baby, c'me on baby, let's dance."

She pulled her arm away from his grasp.

"What's up with you?"

"I've never danced before. Not like this anyway." She looked down at her feet as if this was all their fault.

"There's nothing to it. You look silly for awhile and then you get better."

"No, it just doesn't feel right, not yet."

Jay frowned.

"When it's right, I'll know. But, for now, I just wanna soak it all in. You understand, don't you?"

"No, but it's your path to walk," he said, then sauntered away to join the dancers.

"That Eartha Kit ... if I was only a few hundred years younger ..." she heard Grandfather's voice as he sat down beside her at the fire. "That's why I'm late, that and a little payback," he told her, flashing his mischievous grin. "Did I miss anything?"

"There haven't been any trains yet, if that's what you mean," Angeline told him.

"... and won't likely be any for awhile anyway," he informed her. "But that doesn't mean tomorrow's news won't be interesting."

"What's happening?" she asked, perking up.

"I've said too much, and it hasn't even happened yet. I can't tell you any more."

"You're a tease," she accused him.

They fell silent, Angeline staring into the glowing coals in the fire.

"Can you really see things that are going to happen?" she asked him, transfixed by the pulsating orange afterglow.

"Some, why?"

"I've always been able to see things, ever since I was a kid. Used to scare the hell out of my mother. But most of the things I see are about other people. I haven't got a clue about what's going to happen to me," she said. "Can you see what's going to happen for me?"

"Trains, great lakes, and the bounce of croquet balls. Those things are easy. What goes on in the heart isn't as easy. But I think you already knew that." He settled back, closed his eyes and seemed to be slipping into the rhythm of the drums. Then his eyes popped open and he looked at Angeline with that sense of curiosity that resembles a child delighted with some small, new discovery. "Do you know anything about the World Wide Web?"

IX. Reflected Light

In a darkened room, a young man, probably in his mid-teens, with long black hair tied back into a braid, sat bathed in the blue light of a computer screen. The sound of clicking computer keys punctuated an occasional beep from the computer.

"There's e-mail," he announced over his shoulder, the way a family member calls out to someone he knows is within shouting distance but not in sight. After the sound of approaching footsteps, another face appeared in the technological aura.

"What is it?" Norm asked. His interest in technology had been planted during his tenure in the army. So had his interest in the dark. He was used to covert operations carried out with the aid of night-vision goggles.

His son's interest in technology came naturally.

"It's information about that Netherton guy. Looks like he's pulled a few in New Zealand. He's not to be trusted, it says," the boy summarized.

"Who's it from," Norm asked.

"Uh ... it just says 'Grandfather'?"

X. Bad Timing

In the dark night, in the nearby city of Ashland, under the shadow of an unused coal dock that rose two stories above the highway, bright red flashing lights suddenly sprang to life and guard rails dropped, blocking non-existent traffic from crossing a set of street-level rails. A single headlight beam lit the rails, followed closely by the lonely wail of a train's warning horn, a mating call that went unanswered.

The train slowly rumbled across the highway the way an alcoholic father intrudes on his family's life, expecting everyone to rearrange their lives around his addiction: There are a lot of warning signs but don't expect him to change course for your sake.

An entourage of coal cars followed closely behind the dual engines, but before the train cleared the highway, a single rail slipped from its place and the lead engine veered slightly from the gravel grade, slowing to a reluctant stop, iron wheels digging deeply into the earth. There were moments of time in suspension, as there must be when unexpected violence has happened, dust settling while the engine slipped into a low idle. Then, a door on the engine opened and a man swung out, descending a metal ladder while trying to balance a flashlight in his dominant hand.

As he neared the bottom step, he jumped down and immediately began walking the length of the engine, flashing light at the steel wheels now almost invisible, they had sank so deeply into the moist summer ground.

He looked the length of the engine and then one more time as if hoping for some form of denial to seize him, then put his hands on his hips, disgusted.

“Damnation!”

Chapter Seven

I. The Patron Saint of Irony

Angeline slept late the next morning, almost too late.

On her way to Tom's Burned Down Cafe for a morning cup of coffee, she barely had time to glance over her shoulder to see what color the lake was. Today it was bright blue with choppy waves and an occasional whitecap curling onto the beach. That meant warm and active water. Something was going to happen today. She realized she might not be wearing the right colors for it.

She took the morning newspaper out from under Tom's elbow. The front-page picture depicted a train engine with its iron wheels sunk into the gravel grade. The engine had derailed while hauling coal from the Ashland dock. It was a small derailment, as derailments went. No spilled coal threatened the ecosystem. Emergency response teams did not rush to the site. There was no cataclysm.

Instead, there was irony and irony

was often more important to a culture's good health than cataclysm. This was the same stretch of track railroad officials had pointed to as a prime example of how safe the line through the reservation must be, since both were on the "same maintenance schedule."

She almost felt sorry for the railroad. You can fight politics. You can fight bad press, but you can't fight a universe striving to regain its balance.

"Bad timing," she commented.

"Must be a conspiracy," Tom deadpanned.

Angeline set the newspaper aside and refilled her own coffee cup. She didn't realize she was absent-mindedly fingering her Bone Donor Card until Tom pointed it out.

"You've met Orchid," he noted, nodding toward her hands.

"Yeah. She seems like an interesting person," Angeline answered.

"She's more than that. She's a powerful medicine woman. There's a lot more to her than meets the eye," he said, his voice dropping almost to a whisper. He held her gaze long enough for her to understand that the word "important" might have been an understatement.

Ursula and Glenda chose that moment to make an entrance. Angeline wasn't surprised to find either of them at Tom's. She was surprised only when the two women walked directly behind the bar and began putting on aprons.

"If this is a convention I can't imagine what the theme is," Angeline said.

"I want you to meet my new bartender," Tom said, wrapping an arm around Glenda's shoulders, "and my new archeologist," he added, his remaining arm draped around Ursula's shoulders. "Or is it the other way around?"

"Lucky for you, Tom, it's a nurturing universe or you'd be in real trouble," Ursula told him. "Actually, I have the degree and Glenda has the field experience and neither one of us can mix an Old Fashioned, but at least we can clean up this mess back here." She made the kind of face that said Tom's mess was formidable but she was up to the challenge.

The two women were probably very good at cleaning up messes, in a figurative sense, Angeline surmised.

"Have you been to the tracks yet?" Angeline asked.

"Not yet. I've been busy chasing a personal demon and Glenda's been rebuilding the engine on her Jeep."

Which might have explained why Angeline was drawn so magnetically to the Island. These two women, Tom included for that matter, were misfits in a politically correct society as much as Angeline's life was a jigsaw puzzle, and if Angeline's edges were cut irregularly, then this might be one of the few places she fit. Glenda had spent eighteen months living in a tent once, toughing out winter behind canvas. Angeline still had several months to go before she could top that.

Besides accommodating misfits, the Island satisfied Angeline's considerable and exotic needs and always at the right time.

It gave her a sense of belonging when she needed it, or she could be alone if that was the call from her heart. The Island challenged her at those moments when struggle was good for her soul. She got laid as often as she needed, though not as often as she wanted, and that was probably the better option. And the surrounding lake offered different hues of blue, something she could calibrate with every day, sometimes more often than that.

The best example was the three sets of clothes she carried in the back of her Suzuki. You never knew when the wind would shift and you'd need to change into something warmer, something colder, or something with green in it.

There was pathos. There was comedy. There was never a shortage of irony.

"Have you heard the latest?" Tom asked, returning from a conversation with another late afternoon customer. "The Rev. Olson has taken up miniature golf. They'll probably find burial sites under the golf course now."

II. An Equaysayway Moment

Equaysayway, or Traveling Woman, converted to Catholicism out of love — love of her family.

There were similarities to Pocahontas and John Smith: Michel Cadotte came from a background far different from Equaysayway. He was the future, not the traditional path. But, he was kind-hearted.

There were differences, too. Equaysayway didn't save Michel Cadotte's life. He might have saved hers, and several family members, using the considerable wealth of his income from the North West Fur Company to support her family until his death. He died penniless.

Half-French and half-Indian, Michel Cadotte didn't simply sleep with the girl and then move on, as so many voyageurs before him. He married her.

In order for that to happen, Equaysayway had to join the church. That meant changing her name. As a kind of consolation prize, White Crane, apparently not one to miss an opportunity, insisted that the Island be named for her. If you're going to join the enemy in his camp you might as well get him to name it after you.

Andy Warhol retrospective.

Madeline became a poster girl for the Catholic Church. If it was good enough for Madeline, isn't it good enough for you? It was like the U.S. Army recruiting office displaying Polaroids of local high school seniors who've signed on the dotted line.

That was the myth. The truth was probably far different, Angeline speculated. Equaysayway seemed to Angeline like a practical girl. If the future meant establishing ties with the invading barbarians, so be it. Maybe she was in love with him. Maybe she was just grateful he was kind-hearted and generous. A girl could do a whole lot worse. If that meant becoming the cause celebre' of the Catholic Church, then she could live with that. Who knew the legend would outlive her?

"My life is almost the antithesis of Madeline Cadotte's," Angeline said to Ben, making herself an avocado sandwich in the kitchen at The Restaurant before officially considering herself on duty.

"She embraced the Catholic Church, I rejected it. She married for security, I changed my mind at the last minute. Her name means Traveling Woman. I'm looking for a place where my Suzuki can rust in peace. She had children ... I don't want to think about that. I even turned down being a poster child."

"Your heart?" Ben intoned, indicating he was half-listening, which was more than usual.

"No, the orphanage wanted a happy family photo, the kind that would encourage other Minnesota white couples to consider an Indian girl," she said. "My mother said 'no.' She was willing to raise me, but she didn't see any reason to advertise it."

Business was slow that afternoon and Ben sent her home early. As she walked along the highway toward her campground home, a car pulled up alongside her, moving slowly as if the driver had a different perspective of time. Orchid was behind the wheel. Someone else sat in the back seat. Orchid brought the older model Chevrolet to a stop, and even that was slow. Angeline pulled open the passenger side door and leaned in.

"We're going to the tribal land on the north end, me and my mother," she nodded toward the back seat where the older woman sat, wrapped in a heavy red Pendleton blanket. "Want to come along? We're putting down spirit plates for our ancestors. Yours too."

Angeline didn't respond right away. She'd been struck by the words, 'Yours, too.'

"Mine, too," she repeated, and climbed in. As they slowly gathered speed, without ever gathering much, Angeline glanced behind her at the ancient woman. There was a touch of class in a woman who sat in the back seat while someone else drove. The old woman pulled the blanket closer around her shoulders.

"Nice blanket," Angeline said to either Orchid or her mother, hoping one of them would answer. Orchid spoke up.

"You know why Anishinabe always use red blankets?" Orchid asked. Then she looked back at mother and back at Angeline, covering a shy smile with her hand. "Oh, my mother doesn't talk much. She says, when she says anything, that I talk enough for both of us."

"I always thought that silence was a sign of wisdom. What about red blankets?"

"Back in the day when the army traded supplies with the tribes, they would give us blankets – red blankets from the Canadian army and yellow blankets from the U.S. Army. One winter the U.S. Army tried to move all the Ojibwe out of Wisconsin to Minnesota. They said we had to go all the way to Minnesota to get our annual payment. It was a bad winter and many people got sick and died on the trip there, and even more on the way back. They say the army put sickness in the blankets on purpose. That's why you don't see many yellow blankets on the reservation."

"I use quilts, Norwegian quilts," Angeline responded. "My dad was Norwegian. My mother German. That's how I ended up Catholic. He changed his religion for her." Another Madeline antithesis, Angeline noted. "Not my real parents, though."

Orchid turned off the main road and onto a gravel road, dust swirling around them.

"Why did you touch my heart, the other day?" Angeline asked, remembering the soft, delicate pressure.

"I saw you hurting there," Orchid explained. "I wanted to know why."

"Is that why you rubbed your finger in tobacco first?" Angeline asked. Orchid nodded.

"What was the diagnosis?"

"That was for me, so I would know. You already know, don't you?"

Angeline looked away. "Maybe I do."

Orchid turned off the gravel road and onto a dirt, one-lane pathway. She stopped the car and shut off the motor.

"We have to stop here and walk the rest of the way," Orchid explained. "Sometimes he puts boards in the road with nails in them. We don't want flat tires."

"Who?"

"There's an old man who has a house up here. He doesn't like Indians, so he tries to keep us away from the burial grounds. It's all tribal land, but the tribe leased part of it to him and others. They built houses there and now he thinks he owns all the land. Same old story."

Orchid climbed out of the car, removing Tupperware from behind the seat, handing one of the bowls to Angeline. They left Orchid's mother behind in the car as they walked along the trail.

"My mother used to help me, but

it's too dangerous for her now. I don't want to scare you, but we have to be careful. No telling what could happen."

They walked on in expectant silence. The woods were beautiful, not silent but filled with soothing sounds of wind, creaking branches, small animals and birds. Still, Angeline was on alert. She half expected a bear to jump out into their way.

The path turned away from the woods and onto the beach. They walked through the deep sand, waves sliding in and washing their feet. To their right was a large, two-story house. Angeline shivered when she looked at it, convinced it was looking back at them. They were headed toward another wooded area, and were almost there, when the stillness was interrupted by an angry voice.

"What the hell are you doing back here?!"

They turned. An old man, his anger riding his entire face, his eyebrows forced downward, his fist clenched and beating against the air, stood on the house’s wooden back step.

“Didn’t I tell you never to come back?!”

Suddenly, two dogs, Dobermans, rushed out of the house and broke toward the two women at a full run, barking loudly, their faces mimicking their owner's anger.

“You damn Indians and your superstitions. I told you never to come back!”

Orchid and Angeline looked at each other. Yep, Angeline realized, they were both scared. Running didn't seem like the answer. She looked around the beach. No apparent weapons handy. What to do? She had to decide fast. The dogs were eating up the distance between them with focused intent. As the younger of the two women, and street-wise, she felt responsible for Orchid. Yet, as it turned out, street smarts didn’t mean a damn thing here. Orchid did the unexpected. She turned her back to the dogs and bent over. Angeline took her cue and did the same.

The dogs skidded to a halt, apparently confused, then slowly stepped closer, the better to sniff at these intruders. Then Orchid slowly turned around and exposed her neck. Angeline followed suit. The dogs sniffed some more, and then sat, allowing themselves to be petted.

“And now you turn my own dogs against me!” the angry voice returned. “You damn Indians think you can do anything. This isn’t your Island anymore! Go away!” Then he made one final appeal to the dogs. “Heston! Charleton! C’me on boys!”

But when Orchid and Angeline began walking to the burial grounds, the dogs followed, the angry man’s voice receding into the background like pattern baldness.

“Heathens! Dirty heathens!”

Orchid enlisted Angeline’s help in making spirit plates, bits of food on a white cloth placed at each burial mound. The dogs sat at the perimeter and watched hopefully.

"Not too much," Orchid instructed. "Once it's in the spirit world it expands many, many times, and then comes back to us." Angeline liked that idea. Suddenly a lot of things made sense, a lot of things that had expanded her w o r l d many, many times in life, from friendships to loneliness.

When they were finished, they sat on a rock to finish the rest of the food, sharing it with the Dobermans.

"Are you still angry with your mother?"

"Which one?" Angeline asked sarcastically. Then she thought about the way that sounded. "I'm sorry. Yeah, both of them, probably."

"My mother and me didn't get along for years. She was disappointed in me."

"Why?" Angeline asked incredulously.

"She was a teacher, for many years. She wanted me to be a teacher, too."

"She was a teacher?"

"You wouldn't know it now. She was part of that generation that got taken away from their homes and sent to boarding schools. It was hard on her. They made them take off all their clothes and get deloused and, you know, they came from clean homes. They didn't have any parasites. They were taught to be modest and it hurt to be naked in front of strangers. They cut off their braids and took away their traditional clothes and burned them. They were given rough clothing to wear, like burlap, that gave them sores. If she spoke her own language, they hit her. She still doesn't speak Ojibwe today."

"She still looks angry."

"But she survived, and became a teacher. I think she wanted me to carry on her fight for her. She didn't approve of my learning traditional ways. She thought that world was over. But that's my path. I had to go there, just like she had to go to boarding school."

"And I had to come to the Island," Angeline added, speaking mostly to herself.

"We have to be getting back. My mother's waiting and she doesn't wait too well," Orchid commented.

They took their time walking back, removing their shoes as they strolled along the beach. Orchid, it seemed, couldn't do anything fast. The old man was nowhere to be seen. They dropped the dogs off and returned to the car.

III. Mother-Daughter Moment

Orchid drove her old car back into town, let it roll up in front of The Restaurant and stopped.

"Thanks," Angeline told Orchid, hugging her. "I almost feel like I belong here now."

She pushed the door open and stepped out. Orchid watched her go, up the steps and into the restaurant, then put the car in gear and aimed it toward the ferry dock.

"Are we there yet?" Orchid heard her mother's frail voice from the back of the car. She looked into the rearview mirror. Her mother was still wrapped tightly in the blanket, looking expressionless out the window.

"We've been already, Ma. We're going back now." She spoke loudly and turned slightly to the rear so her mother would be sure to hear her.

Orchid drove onto the ferry dock, got in line behind several other cars waiting for a return trip, put the car in park and turned off the engine.

"You know, I did the best I could for you," her mother said from the backseat.

Orchid pinched her eyes shut, pushing back her feelings. Despite the effort, a tear broke free.

"I know, Ma," she said, her voice breaking, "I know."

IV. Bear Sign

The Restaurant was a happening place that night. Apparently a lot of people needed a little time in hell, as long as they could walk out at will. If they didn't insult Ben, they could come back any time.

When traffic finally slowed around midnight, Glenda arrived. Angeline was surprised to see her there without Ursula. Better Glenda than Ursula, Angeline thought. She wanted to talk, not listen.

"I'm shopping for a new mother. You interested?"

"Well, if my estimation is correct, I would have been about fifteen when you were born. It would have been a virgin birth."

Angeline cracked a smile. Glenda blushed. Angeline wouldn't have to wonder later what she really meant by that.

"You should talk more often. You're better at it than you think."

Glenda blushed all over again, but she went through a complete re-composition routine afterward, smoothing her hair, pursing her lips, clearing her throat, as if she was practiced at it. “Are you sure it’s a mother you’re looking for? You already have more than most people. I don't think that’s how you got your emotional limp.”

And Glenda was more perceptive than Angeline thought. That one hit her where she hid her personal demons.

“I feel as though there’s something I need to do to really make this my home. I feel like I should wash the windows, plant a garden, or die and be buried here. Something that says I’ve left footprints. I had an impact. I marked my scent in strategic places.”

“I understand. When friends come to visit me, and they volunteer to cook dinner or wash the dishes, I let them. It helps them feel at home,” Glenda responded.

“Or, maybe I could cause repercussions,” she mused. “I’m good at that. I can't help it.”

They were interrupted by a clattering sound from the direction of the kitchen and went to investigate. They found garbage cans knocked over in the alley and food scattered about. They also found bear tracks.

"I think I know him," she told Glenda.

Glenda helped Angeline clean up the mess, then left. Angeline locked up the restaurant and started walking home. She'd walked nearly a block before she realized she was following bear tracks.

The tracks took her past Tom's Burned Down Cafe where someone was singing Gordon Lightfoot's *Canadian Railroad Trilogy*.

"There was a time in this fair land when the railroads did not run ..." it began as they approached.

By the time they reached the Island's only miniature golf course, Angeline could hear the words, "... Long before the white man, and long before the wheel ..."

There was someone on the 16th hole, hunched over in the dark. Angeline thought she recognized Equilibrium. It had to be the real Equilibrium. No one was capable of making a duplicate, especially one with windmill arms to bat away golf balls aimed at a strategically located cup. Angeline walked past. She didn't want to disturb the balance.

The bear tracks took her past the street that led down to the ferry dock where a few cars were waiting for the last ride back to the mainland. The last ferry ... Either you made the last ferry or had already figured out where you were spending the night. The ferry added a timely element to propositions. "I have to know now while I can still make the ferry."

The tracks crossed the street and took them to the Madeline Island Museum, through the gate, into the yard and right up to the Spirit Stone, where they stopped.

V. The Totem Island

Making totem Islands was dangerous business, Equilibrium believed.

It was like playing God, a giant god who towered above the lighthouses and breakwater, who left big footprints in artificial turf; or a careless god who could sink the ferry just by stepping in the wrong place. That's why the miniature golf course made her nervous. True, a lot of things made her nervous, but the miniature golf course especially. Who could predict the effect it had on the Island's balance or which human beings, putter in hand, would feel compelled to play god.

It wasn't even historically accurate. Well, it was accurate in one way. Tourists walked all over it without really seeing it. But some of the most important parts of the Island were missing.

There was no Tom's Burned Down Cafe, as if it had really burned down and disappeared.There was no walk-in hell. And there was no Indian Cemetery.

That's why she'd been crouching on the miniature golf course in the middle of the night, cutting small pieces of

Astroturf from the first hole and using those bits and pieces to make burial mounds on the 16th green. She used toothpicks borrowed from The Restaurant to fashion little crosses. She used seashells for headstones. She even found some yellow thread in a bird's nest to simulate plastic tape, to represent the line which stated, "Police barricade — do not cross," just like the plastic tape that now marked the boundary line between the cemetery and the Olson's house. Someone's toy, a plastic Indian lost on the beach, represented the sentry.

Then, next to the place that she thought looked like the museum, she placed a pebble, a small stone, to represent the Spirit Stone.

When she stepped back to examine her work, she thought it was leaning a little. But she couldn't tell for sure. She didn't know which was off balance, the totem cemetery or herself — she had to lean over so far these days just to stay even.

"Now all we need is a bear."

She reached inside a soiled plastic

bag, one she had rescued from a ditch along the road, and pulled out a stuffed bear. The bear had a few miles on him, but was obviously well loved once. She knelt down beside the diorama she'd created and set the bear down beside her representation of the Spirit Stone.

"Well, what would you like to do now?" she asked the bear, then lifted it up to her ear so she could hear his whispers.

"Go for a walk? Sure. Where would you like to go?"

She lifted the bear up one more time.

"To visit Angeline? OK."

She began manipulating the bear's legs until it was near Equilibrium's representation of the campground.

"Oh, she's not home yet. We'll wait."

VI. Hunger Overcomes Symbolism

Angeline built a large fire that night. She had some thinking to do and she did her best thinking when the fire was hot. She thought about the time she almost got married. He wasn't the problem either, not really. That's why they were still friends. That's why they still slept with each other sometimes. He was just the living example of the last time she tried to solve all her problems by pouring gas on the fire.

No, her problems went deeper. She was a woman with a foot in two worlds. Admittedly, there were some advantages. She was invited to twice as many parties. She'd been to the Mall of America (once that she would admit to) and could still build a fair campfire. She could talk as easily with yuppies as she could with ... with ... well, with bears.

But who could she offend in what politically incorrect Halloween costume? What traditional dress would she wear at her wedding? Where was home for the holidays and where would she want her heart buried? When those questions reared up at her, she felt she had no place where she belonged. She became a tribe of one.

She wondered if Madeline had any regrets. Probably, just not the obvious ones, like, 'Why didn't I marry the boy in the lodge next door?' Or maybe, 'Why didn't I use a hyphenated first name?' Madeline-Equaysayway had a kind of ring to it.

She threw another log on the fire, and then two more because it didn't seem big enough.

Of course, she knew she couldn't just put an ad in the paper for a new mother. She already had two, one she didn't want, and the other ... she didn't know if she wanted her or not, and was half-afraid that if she did meet her it would be the same old rejection all over again. Maybe it was better to never know her and live on the hope they could be best buddies if they ever went camping together. At least with genetics there had to be some common ground. She thought about making a pot of coffee but, in her camp, that wasn't as easy as plugging in the Mr. Coffee. Instead, she decided to crawl in between the blankets. Even if she couldn't sleep, she could agonize just as easily when she was snug and warm, maybe even better.

But she did sleep, much to her surprise. Maybe it was best described as a numb kind of trance-like state. That could be a good sign. That could be a bad sign. This night, it was both.

She heard him before she saw him, the same snuffling noises and general disregard for twigs and small branches. It was the sound of the coffee pot, the one she almost filled, crashing to the ground from the picnic table that opened her eyes.

He stood over her, sniffing her at first, then stepped back and made himself large, as large as any fear she'd ever known. Her heart raced out of control, stuttering along the way.

"Who are you?" she asked, only she didn't have to say the words, just think them and knew he would hear her.

"You know," he answered. This time the words didn't have to hang in the air for her to read. She felt them.

"You were going to tell me what I needed to be afraid of."

"You don't have to be afraid of anything. It's what you choose to fear, and you choose to fear me."

He turned to leave.

"Will you be back?"

He didn't answer.

"Will you be back?"

He was gone.

She slowly closed her eyes. She dreamed of the time she was seventeen years old and still living at home. Only she wasn't seventeen in this dream. She was thirty-something. It was early evening. Her mother was at church. She hadn't seen her leave but knew that's where she was. It was where she had run away too often when Angeline was seventeen. Angeline climbed the stairs to the second floor bedroom, her legs getting heavier with each step, her level of stress rising as she ascended, sweat beginning to form on her neck and back. She seemed to grow younger as she climbed, so that by the time she reached the top she was seventeen again. She walked to the bedroom door. Her father was in there. She could feel his presence. She could almost smell him and the illness that was stealing him away a little bit every day. She reached for the doorknob.

"Run!" she heard a voice behind her. She turned and saw a little man, no more than a foot tall. Another little man, maybe three feet in height, stood beside him. "Hurry!" he shouted. She woke up in a sweat, leapt out of bed, Norwegian quilts flying.

She began throwing her belongings into the back of her Suzuki with no regard for order or organization. She didn't bother folding her tent, but pulled it from the ground violently and forced it into her car, the blankets trapped inside, still warm. She fired up the Suzuki and raced from the campground, flying over potholes and speed bumps. She cornered the curves on the road at dangerous speeds, racing to get to the ferry dock. But the last ferry was already pulling out as she arrived. The Suzuki's engine idled on the dock as she sat with her head pressed against the steering wheel. Slowly her heartbeat steadied.

"Shit!"

She was getting closer to the truth, the truth in her life anyway, and that by itself was frightening enough.

VII. Going for a Swim

Equilibrium walked the bear back to the simulated museum.

"I know. That was no fun, but it had to happen," she told the bear. "Where should we go now?"

She lifted the bear up again, listened carefully, a quizzical expression appearing on her face.

"The north end? Why?" The bear lifted his snout to her ear as if whispering a secret. "OK, but we'll have to swim most of the way."

She led the bear to the edge of the

fourteenth hole, and helped him dive off the edge, following him as he swam arm over arm.

VIII. Competitive Spirits

In a tall glass building which helped define the Toronto skyline, on a top floor, in a corner office, a light burned late into the night. Inside the corner office, three men, all in expensive suits, shared a drink. It was late. They could relax a little.

Two of the men sat on a sofa. The other leaned back against a desk, his desk presumably. The two men on the sofa were idea men. Their jobs were to have brainstorms, but to make certain the storms weren't so large they upset the fiscal balance. Their storms had to follow the prevailing winds. They wore power ties, but their ties were a definite tier below. There was a protocol to such displays of status. Like a prairie chicken, if the male's display, if his attempt to attract a female, was too ostentatious it might get the attention of another male instead, a possessive male, an angry male. Unless you were ready to fight, and win, you accepted your role and awaited your time.

“What if we just went through? There’s no barricade,” one of the sofa-men asked the rhetorical question.

“It would be a public relations nightmare. They know what they’re doing. Could you see the ‘film at ten’? A massive diesel engine crushing an Indian stick and eagle feather under its wheels ...” The other sofa-man discounted the idea.

“There’s no linkage with someone we own, someone we can leverage?” the third man asked. He was obviously the highest-ranking chief in this corporate tribe.

“Nothing there either,” the second man responded.

“What do they want?” the CEO asked.

“It’s not a kidnapping. They aren’t holding hostages in exchange for something. Apparently, what they say they want is actually what they want – to protect the water, all that idealistic bullshit."

"There's no other way to transport?" the chief asked.

"Not that much volume, and we need a lot of volume. Nothing else is cost-effective. Volume drives this project."

The highest-ranking chief turned and walked toward the window, or exterior wall which was all glass anyway. He looked outward, then downward. He didn't look down very often. Bad ear. It gave him vertigo. He never understood the affection with this modern architecture, but he didn't write the rules, he only mastered them. He turned and looked at his two brainstormers.

"What if we got to know them, or at least act like we care. Win their trust?"

"We tried talking, but – "

"They've seen bullshit before. They know how it smells."

The CEO turned back to look out

his corner office window. He scanned through his inventory collected from a series of personal improvement workshops. He made it a practice to attend the latest and newest, not for personal self-improve but to be on top of the language others were using at cocktail parties. He filled his idle time finding ways to turn those lessons to his advantage. The sincerity most people brought back with them from the workshops made the trick that much easier.

"The governor is with us. I say we use the National Guard," the first sofa-man suggested.

"Won't work," the CEO countered.

"I bet it does, and I'm willing to back it up, say, with ten dollars," the first man contended.

The CEO turned to the sofa-man and smiled. His competitive spirit was engaged. It wasn't the size of the bet, but the bragging rights.

"I love object lessons." The CEO accepted the gentlemanly wager.

Chapter Eight

I. The Morning After

Angeline drove back to her campsite and slept in the Suzuki the rest of the night, forcing her body into a series of awkward positions to find some way to get comfortable. Or maybe comfort wasn't what she was looking for. If numbness was the goal then sleeping sitting up had numbed one selective part of her body after another. She awoke stiff and sore.

Still, she waited for the coffee to be ready before she started replanting her tent, replacing the smudge pots and replenishing her stock of firewood. With a reasonably secure environment she could call home, a safe place she could return to, she found her sketchpad and pencils and left in search of subject matter. She had a definite subject in mind.

Glenda was bent over the hood of her Jeep, which was parked under a shade tree beside a small cottage located on the Island's eastern shore. Land values were lower on the eastside due to prevailing winds. The worst storms came from the nor'east. There was no storm today, although massive driftwood piled up on the beach stood as testimony to past turmoil. Today, however, Glenda was leaned over the hood of her Jeep, chains reaching up from the engine well to a tree branch over head, and Glenda poised to hoist the engine from its nest.

"I hope you don't mind. I'm a little busy right now," Glenda apologized.

"I hope you don't mind. I'm feeling artistic," Angeline responded, choosing a stump-end with a view of the proceedings. She sat down and began sketching.

Angeline hadn't chosen art so much as it had chosen her. Even though she knew all the words for most feelings, there were times when no word could describe what she felt. That's where art came into play. Art gave definition to feelings that had no words. It gave her a chance to work at a pace that suited her. If a stray feeling emerged that demanded some processing, she could give it the time it needed.

"Have you seen many women rebuild an engine before?" Glenda asked as she worked.

"It kind of reminds me of my dad. He used to escape to the garage to work on his car when my mother got to be too much for him," Angeline answered, drawing a few reference points on the paper.

"Did you draw pictures of him?"

"A few, but most of those were in crayon. He died when I was seventeen, before I got serious about art."

Glenda climbed under the Jeep, taking a big wrench with her, lying on her back to disconnect the engine's lifelines.

"What did he die from?" Her voice sounded subdued, muffled by the surrounding sheet metal.

"A tumor in his head. My mother didn't take the whole thing very well. She got more religious than ever, like she wasn't already. I think it scared her more than it did him," Angeline said. She sketched the mechanic leaning so far into the engine well that her head wasn't visible. There was a tension in that pose, like a lion trainer sticking his head into a lion's mouth. She'd sooner trust a lion than a V-6. "I had to take care of my dad, mostly. I wasn't afraid of being around it ... dying that is. I never have been afraid of death. Living's been a hell of a challenge, though."

Angeline flipped the page and started another sketch of Glenda flat on her back under her Jeep, her legs spread wide while wrestling with some nut or bolt.

"We had some good conversations, my dad and me, before he died and when he wasn't hurting too much," Angeline said.

"About what?"

"Oh, the war. My dad fought in World War Two. He was in D-Day and the liberation of Paris."

"A real hero, eh?"

"He never saw it that way. Just a scared kid, you know? Or a deer caught in the headlights. His whole life was a lot like that. He knew and pretty much took everything in stride."

"He sounds more honest than your mom. How did they meet? They ever tell you?"

"Before the war. Nothing dramatic. I mean, there wasn't any moonlight at the oasis or anything. I think she just had him pegged for someone who would play the role, work his nine-to-five and not play around or anything. That's pretty much all he wanted when he got back from the war."

Angeline flipped the page, stood and moved to a new spot where she could gain a different perspective.

"You know what he told me before he died? I just remembered this," she said, this time drawing Glenda's face in the shadows beneath the Jeep.

"What?"

"He said, 'God isn't who your mother thinks he is.' Isn't that a strange thing to say?"

"I don't know. What was the context?"

Angeline took a deep breath, leaned back and looked up at the sunny sky, trying to remember. It was the first time she'd ever heard him contradict her mother, and it was when he was close, very close, like death had to push him into a corner, or tear another page off the calendar, to squeeze it out of him.

"We were talking about the war, about how he thought, when he first got over there, that if he was a good soldier, that would make all the difference. Then he would make it back alive," she said, still staring at the sky and streaks of clouds stretched across it. "But then he said he saw enough good soldiers get blown into smaller pieces that he knew, that wasn't it. It had nothing to do with any kind of good, not good soldier, good person or good cause."

Glenda crawled out from under the Jeep, leaned back against it and listened, still holding the wrench in her hand.

"'Your mother,' he said, 'thinks that if you're good you won't get as much pain. But pain is just a part of it no matter what.' After awhile, he just started to think that his life was a movie and however much he wanted to change parts of it, he couldn't. But once he realized he was sitting in the front row watching, it got easier somehow."

Angeline looked at Glenda, hoping for a reaction.

"Is that the way you want it? Easier?"

"Even if I did, it's not what I got."

"Give me a hand with this engine."

Angeline left her sketchpad and pencil on the grass and walked over to the Jeep. She helped Glenda disconnect the hood and the two of them lifted it and leaned it against the house.

"Now, I'll hoist the block and tackle and you make sure it clears the engine well," Glenda instructed.

To Angeline, it seemed like heart surgery. She wondered if Glenda would do her next.

II. Love Lost

The Rev. Olson sat by his window, the one with the lace curtains that overlooked the cemetery. He rested his elbows on the windowsill and his chin on his hands. He was sulking. He missed his croquet.

He tried to test the waters once, to see if the storm had died down, but while he was still setting up the wickets, a bus pulled in and it was all he could do to get to the house without being harassed out of his being. He had to cover his head like a common criminal while flashbulbs went off all around him.

Here he sat by his window as if he was under house arrest. What crime had he committed? It was just a bad bounce of the ball, that's all. His intentions had been good. Didn't good intentions count for anything? Unless ...

He couldn't help but think about it as a message from God. The humility thing was obvious, maybe too obvious. Once he publicly confessed, in front of the TV cameras, to letting his ego carry him away, things only got worse. Now he was practically a celebrity. He was becoming some kind of symbol for those who believed the Indians should just shut up and assimilate, and those same people told him so with righteous enthusiasm, then became bored with him when he tried to explain his point of view – it was just a bad bounce.

But it was the passion for the game that he missed the most. There weren't many things in his life he could get passionate about – a little competitive fun with his grandchildren and lemonade on a warm summer afternoon. That was about it.

Well, there was one other thing. There was the girl, the messenger. He still remembered what she had told him.

"There's a big imbalance coming." She was right about that. Still, it wasn't the words that stuck with him. To be honest, it was her breasts. If he let his mind wander, and he often did, that's where it landed. It was getting so he didn't trust his imagination. He could see every detail of those small, pointed breasts, with nipples that seemed disproportionately large. He could see their every movement, extrapolating changes of shape with her every motion. He could even gauge their volume, and what little space they displaced, all in his mind. In his fantasies, he could see her, mallet in hand, leaning over, taking aim at the croquet ball, the tank top T-shirt falling away from her chest, and she would glance up at him before swinging, asking his permission with a look whether to send his ball for a ride. Where was the message from God in all of that, trading a guiltless passion for passion of another kind altogether?

Well, he'd had his fill. He was going out to some place public and he didn't care what anyone thought about it, least of all God. He found a pair of sunglasses one of his grandchildren had left behind. They didn't exactly fit his style, what with the day-glow green frames and rose-colored lenses, but they would have to do. Then, he found an old trench coat and a stocking hat, put on both and left his self-imposed exile.

III. The Gallery

Angeline went straight to work at The Restaurant from Glenda's shade tree garage, carrying her sketchpad under her arm as she sauntered into The Island Restaurant. Ursula was enjoying an afternoon cup of coffee and insisted on seeing the drawing.

"Oh, my," Ursula gushed, with her heavy Germanic accent. "You've captured her just right. You see, my dear, with Glenda you must place her in context just so. Otherwise, you might miss her most endearing traits altogether. Where will you hang it?"

"Hang it?"

"Surely you must show this. I suggest that wall over there." Ursula pointed to the wall where the Island kids hung their dreamscapes.

"Ben will kill me."

"He'll do no such thing."

Angeline was taken back by Ursula's confidence.

"How do you know?"

"Because, you are an artist and you won't let him."

Angeline smiled. Ursula was right, of course, and now Angeline knew it. She held it against the wall in various locations until Ursula approved, then called for thumbtacks, affixing it in place where it caught just the right light from a table candle. Then she stepped back and admired her work. She felt like an artist now, for the first time ever.

IV. A Day Trip to Hell

Angeline's first thought, when she saw the Day-Glow green sunglasses, stocking hat and trench coat was that a robber had decided to stop for lunch on his way to the Island Savings and Loan. Only when he slipped into a table in a dark corner did she think "celebrity" and "can the paparazzi be far behind?" There is celebrity and then there's celebrity ... On the Island, local celebrity would more likely get you more free drinks than land you on the cover of "People" magazine.

When she looked closely, she recognized the Rev. Olson from his ample abdomen and the expression of a condemned man on his features. He avoided all eye contact and hid behind his menu. On the other hand, he sat at the table near her drawing, so that had to mean something. She went to the table to take his order. She couldn't help but wonder what would bring a minister to this Walk-in-Hell.

"What can I get you?" she asked, her pad and pencil poised. "I guess I hadn't really thought that out. I'm still surprised that I got this far," he answered.

"I can get you a cup of coffee while you're deciding."

"I'm not really a coffee kind of man. I was thinking, um, more like lemonade. Do you have real lemonade here, made from scratch, or the mix kind?"

Angeline smiled to herself. She knew all the symptoms. A lot of people came into the restaurant just because it had been an eternity since they'd shared a little talk with someone they didn't even know.

"I think I can find a couple lemons in the back. It might take awhile, though. I hope you don't mind waiting?"

"I've got lots of time, time enough to ... to ... to look at the drawings."

V. The Critic

When Ben saw the new drawing hanging on the wail of his restaurant he had to see it from close range, judge it and react without thinking. He felt he had the right to approve of any new additions to the Walk-in-Hell and Art Gallery, not because he owned the restaurant, but because he viewed himself as Hell's art critic. For this to really be Hell, there were certain standards that must be maintained.

Ben approached the new addition with caution, put on a pair of reading glasses, and examined the drawing closely. He leaned in to view the details. He stepped back to take in the full effect, all the while oblivious to the hunched up little man in the green sunglasses. Then, Ben issued his opinion.

"What the hell is this?!"

Angeline, who was busy in the kitchen adding sugar to her lemonade concoction, heard him bellow, and knew exactly what he was referring to. She entered the dining room, her attitude adjusted for confrontation, slamming the doors open wide, and loudly, for full effect. She knew it would get his immediate attention, as often as he yelled at the help for slamming doors. He turned on her. Their eyes locked.

"Is this yours?" he demanded to know, removing his reading glasses and pointing them in the general direction of her drawing, almost hitting the Rev. Olson more than once. The Rev. Olson had to dodge and duck to keep from getting hit. Angeline almost felt sorry for the man. He couldn't go anywhere, even to Walk-in-Hells, without falling into the spotlight. But when Angeline looked at Ben, she saw something else altogether — she saw an archetypical gatekeeper. She saw the kind of person who believed he had the right to decide who received invitations to which exclusive parties, who was allowed to join which segregated country club or who would become the accuser in which political scandal. Their ranks included most idle gossipers, those who set the community standards for morality and all art critics. Angeline knew how to deal with this. She'd been dealing with her mother all her life.

"Lighten up, Ben. The way you smoke, you don't have the stamina to sustain a really good outrage anymore," she told him.

"This is a wall where truth is shown. What makes you think you even know the truth?"

"Oh! So you have a monopoly on the truth," she scoffed, walking toward him, brandishing a lemonade. He kept a wary eye on the lemonade as she approached. "Open up to the possibility that every moral judgment doesn't have to be issued from the court of the nineteen-sixties. Even you must have learned something new since then. As for the truth, I'll give you some of mine. The truth is this is art," she said, sweeping her lemonade hand toward the drawing, spilling only a little on the Rev. Olson. "I am an artist." She swept her hand back, baptizing the Rev. Olson a bit more. "And that's a wall for displaying art. It stays. Get over it."

She placed the half-glass of lemonade on the table in front of the Rev. Olson and walked away to applause from the restaurant patrons, leaving Ben mentally regressing back to the Sixties.

Chapter Nine

I. The Wooden Indian

Norm pulled his 1974 Oldsmobile to the curb outside Ashland City Hall and turned off the engine. The cylinders rolled once or twice more before the engine stopped. Norm preferred driving cars built in the mid-seventies, in part from habit and partly for practical considerations.

Before he was hired as photographer for the tribal newspaper, the only cars he could afford were built during the American car industry's low-water mark. Dealers practically gave them away. That was before computerized circuits and fuel injection. If his Oldsmobile broke down, Norm could do most of the work himself and find all the spare parts he needed at junkyards. And with all that heavy gauge sheet metal, he felt safer on the roads. It was like riding in the armored personnel carriers during his days in Panama. You didn't get there real fast, but you could clear your own highway if you had to.

On top that, he liked the legroom.

He was a few minutes late for the meeting, but it wasn't as if he really cared about what they were saying. He just wanted them to know he was watching.

He checked to make sure he had his press pass. He carried it with him everywhere. His Veteran's Administration card was the only other I.D. with more mileage on it.

He liked his job. It was better than working at the casino. It gave him room to maneuver, to annoy and to irritate, that and the freedom to operate within his own sphere of influence. Nobody at the tribal offices really knew anything about photography so he didn't have to worry about second level administrators telling him what to do and how to do it. To get them off his back, it was usually enough to ask how tight they wanted the picture's grain. That usually shut them up.

He climbed out of his car and slammed the door, twice. The frame was sagging and the doors didn't fit the way they used to.

He was halfway across the street before realizing he'd left his camera under the seat. He wouldn't need it, he decided. He mostly shot nature scenes anyway and there was nothing natural about this meeting.

He climbed the steps to the imposing front door. The building had been erected by the federal government to regulate such things as mining, lumbering and quarrying. It had been the official administrative building for raping and pillaging the land.

He pulled open the imposing City Hall door and entered, finding himself confronted with another wide, wooden, imposing flight of stairs. He shook his head. White people had a thing for stairs, especially in public buildings as if, after centuries of practice, they had mastered the art of forcing supplicants to look up. Or maybe it was a test, like the Rainbow Family gathering in Northeast Minnesota where he'd shot photos a few years earlier. The Rainbow Family was a 1970s mostly white tribe born out of the 1960s. They held a gathering of members, locals and the perpetually curious, each year in a different state. Norm had been curious about any group calling itself a tribe. The annual gathering was always held deep in the forest, usually requiring a walk of several miles through rugged country. It was a test, he was told, to determine how badly each person wanted to be there. The walk damn near killed him, or least had him seriously thinking about giving up cigarettes. With this meeting, they could have chosen some place deep in the national forest. He climbed the stairs two at a time.

This gathering couldn't be mistaken for something tribal. The Wisconsin Department of Natural Resources sent appropriate, mid-level representatives to confer with their appropriate counterparts from the Environmental Protection Agency, the mining company and the railroad. He was late, but he knew they would need a few minutes to sort out whose hands were how deep in whose pockets.

At the top of the stairs, Norm found himself at the end of a long hallway. In the Bible of architectural intimidation, Norm thought, long hallways had to be in the same chapter as wide, imposing stairs. The meeting room was at the end of the hall behind another heavy wooden door firmly closed. In the other direction, standing next to the elevator was a full-sized cigar store wooden Indian. It was almost as if the Indian was waiting stoically for the elevator. Norm smiled. There were times, he knew, when the white man didn't realize how idiotic he appeared, especially when it came to advertising icons.

"Why didn't you tell me there was an elevator?" Norm asked the wooden Indian, as if accusing him of disloyalty to his race.

Norm turned to his right and strode down the hallway. He pulled against the heavy conference room door and entered. Those inside, dressed in an odd-lot collection of suits and uniforms, stopped talking and looked up at him. Norm knew some of the men and could guess at the rest.

"This meeting is closed to the

public," one man in a suit said, obviously trying to be firm but not threatening. It was a skill Norm had never mastered. When he was being firm, he wanted to be threatening. Norm didn't know the suit, but knew of him. He was a troubleshooter from the governor's office. He also recognized the railroad's imported negotiator from New Zealand. You couldn't miss a hat like that, even in a Fourth of July parade.

"How can it be closed?" Norm asked.

"Contract negotiations," was the terse reply.

"What contract?"

"Mining contract. According to a recent attorney general's opinion ..." he began, reaching for a piece of paper resting at his elbow, "governmental agencies have the right to – "

"All right," Norm cut him off. "You don't have to read the whole damn thing." He turned and left.

But he didn't leave the building,

not immediately. He walked to the end of the hall and paced in front of the wooden Indian. For a few moments he thought about staying, waiting in the hallway until the meeting was over. Then he could confront them. He looked into the wooden Indian's face.

"What do you think?" There was no answer. "You're right, I'm becoming too predictable."

Next to the wooden Indian, on a clean white wall, was a framed newspaper story providing historical information. *At least it wasn't painted on one of those damn, brown historical markers,* he thought.

'At one time,' it said, 'Ashland boasted a flourishing cigar industry. Hand-rolled cigars with an Ashland label enjoyed a nationwide reputation. This wooden Indian was located in front of one of the city's premier cigar stores around the turn of the century.' Norm frowned. He removed a felt-tip black marker from his pocket and wrote a message on the clean white wall under the framed newspaper story. 'And at one time all of Ashland belonged to the Ojibwe nation.’

He smiled again. There was nothing like correcting history to make you feel like you’ve done something worthwhile with your morning, he thought.

II. More Sulfuric Acid

Ray Cadotte had arrived at the meeting just early enough to pour a cup of coffee for himself and choose a seat in the background where he could watch with detached amusement. Ray didn’t look forward to these kinds of meetings, though he had to admit he admired the government's specifications for coffee. Because this was an interdepartmental meeting, the federal government’s specs took precedence over the state’s and the federal government had higher standards.

Ray had worked for the state Department of Natural Resources almost fifteen years now. He was used mostly as liaison on tribal fishing regulations. It was a role he’d inherited. His great-great-

great-grandfather on his mother's side of the family, Ben Armstrong, had once operated the trading post on Madeline Island early in the nineteenth century, a post his great-great-great-grandfather on his father's side, Michel Cadotte, had founded.

Whenever the government had difficulties with the Ojibwe, they'd hold a meeting, invite Ray along, ask his advice and then ignore it, satisfied that they had solicited the Ojibwe perspective. That was typical of the government's approach, no matter what their specs were for coffee.

They assumed that one voice, regardless of the minority involved, spoke for all. Ray had at least three voices just inside of him — one when he spoke with other government employees, one when he spoke to other tribal members, and a third when he was just trying to get laid.

"The tribal council denies it has any linkage with these radicals," a railroad representative said. "If we can't find linkage maybe we should fast-forward to leverage."

Ray had some understanding of leverage — leverage, repercussions and sulfuric acid. It was Armstrong who had helped the Ojibwe Tribe negotiate the Treaty of 1854. For his efforts, the tribe insisted that one square mile of land be set aside for Ben. The land included most of the City of Ashland. Ben never had the chance to enjoy it. One winter night, as he was returning from the treaty negotiations, a stranger ran through camp where he and some friends had set up for the night. The stranger threw acid in his face. He lost his eyesight. It didn't take a leap of faith to figure out it was an act of retribution for Armstrong's role in the treaty negotiations. Unable to work, he signed a contract turning the whole plot over to developers, but was swindled out it by land speculators.

"You spoke with the governor, I presume," the railroad representative said, turning to the governor's man.

"There's not much to go on there," the governor's man answered.

Which was the moment Norm

decided to enter the room. Talk about a conversation killer. Ray met Norm's eye and nodded slightly. He'd fill him in afterward on the turn of events, closed meeting or not. He was relieved when Norm didn't opt for a confrontation. Confrontations, Ray believed, were nearly as tiresome as the typical bureaucratic pace when closed meetings neared the lunch hour. Norm left and they all turned back to the railroad man.

"What about jobs here? What if we put together a track maintenance crew and hired men from the tribe?" the railroad representative asked.

All eyes were directed at Ray, prompting his opinion.

"What? And quit jobs at the tribal conservation office, or with casino security or as tribal judge? Too late for that," he said, hoping they noted the edge of sarcasm in his voice.

"I say it's time for a show of force," the mining representative said. "We've talked before about using the National Guard. I think this is the time."

"That would be a grave mistake." All eyes turned in Netherton's direction. "There is always a temptation to think of aboriginal cultures in simplistic terms, especially when you don't understand them. But these cultures have been conducting complex negotiations for more centuries than we have, and they're better at it. Face it. They hold all the cards. Worse yet, they know it. You can't begin to form a workable strategy until you can see that."

"They hold all the cards? What cards?" the mining representative asked with undisguised incredulity. "We have more resources, more lawyers, more numbers any way you look at it. What have they got?"

"The high moral ground and public opinion. That cancels anything you can muster. Better still, they have dual citizenship. When it suits their purposes, they can play the system better than you. When it doesn't, they can claim tradition. You can't beat that."

The mining representative, feeling the frustration of a child with a new toy he isn’t allowed to use, leaped to his feet. “Weren’t you supposed to get around that by building some kind of trust?”

“There's only one kind of trust, the kind built on honesty,” Netherton said calmly. “Apparently they were tipped off by three hundred years of bad faith.”

III. Changes

The Lumber Baron Cafe sat across the street from the Ashland City Hall. Norm hadn’t been there in years, not since he’d returned from Panama. His fatigue jacket was newer then. He was still relatively clean-cut, by military standards, and too Gichi-mookomann for tribal standards, as in hair far too short for a braid.

But his hair was still black and his skin was still not white.

They didn’t serve him then. Didn’t talk to him. Didn’t even acknowledge his presence with the obligatory glass of water. He wondered if anything had changed over the years.

He went inside and chose a table near the door.

The sign, “We reserve the right to refuse service to anyone,” still hung behind the counter. Other customers stared at him as he entered. The waitresses, dressed in pastel uniforms and small white aprons, ignored him.

This wasn’t exactly the place where the Aryan Nation held its weekly past-presidents brunches, and it might not have been where the neo-Nazis held their annual achievement awards banquet, but the clientele were the same ones who gave aid and comfort. Some things never change.

Some things had.

Norm’s hair was long, tied into a tight braid, and had streaks of gray in it. There was a New Age store located across the street. He could see it through the plate glass window. But mostly, he had changed.

He joined the U.S. Army because his options were limited. He really did want to see the world not necessarily exotic ports of call, but anything which wasn't the reservation. He discovered Panama, and other Central American places where armed camps defined the borders. The experience had opened his eyes.

He watched while Americans operated with impunity, serving the country's "vital national interests," arming anyone who drove a Chevrolet and drank Coke.

It wasn't as if he'd been wandering around Central America as an American techno-ninja, viewing the Third World through night-vision goggles, killing with abandon. Assassination was designed to make a point, send a message. Too much killing was bad for business. The CIA and the mafia — twins separated at birth.

He left the army thinking there was little point in standing up to the public-private partnership the U.S. military had formed with the large corporate boards. This wasn't a point of view he'd arrived at easily. It had taken years before his perspective had evolved.

There was no one incident that had

changed his mind. More than anything, he began to see the game played out. The results weren't as predictable as the military analysts had led him to believe.

Sure, there were conspiracies everywhere. But the closer he looked the more those conspiracies appeared like situation comedies. Almost no one stayed in the game long enough to pass "Go" and collect two hundred dollars. Today's friends became tomorrow's Darth Vaders. Former friendly presidents in Panama and Iraq came to mind.

Iron Curtains fell and Russian premiers lost power without dying first. American presidents won wars and lost re-elections, or at least one did. Other presidents got hum-jobs in the Oval Office or were elected with fewer votes than their opponent. It was almost enough to motivate him to run for office, at least for the hum-job part.

And the federal court said the Ojibwe people could fish in the ceded territory off the reservation. That was a starting point for the tribe, in the modern era anyway. Today the Ogichidaa were blockading the railroad tracks, trying to save themselves and their white neighbors from mining folly. But they were only a few years removed from the federal court rulings that gave the Ojibwe Tribes the right to gather resources again in northern Wisconsin.

Norm went fishing once, elbowing his way past the angry mobs of white anglers carrying signs with racial slurs like, "Spear an Indian, Save a walleye." In the minds of sport fishermen, spearing a female walleye pike during spawning season was worse than abortion. Never mind that the Ojibwe milked the captured females for spawn and raised them in hatcheries where they stood a better chance of survival than in open water.

Norm saw incensed white men and women at the boat landings carrying spears with Indian babies in effigy, pierced by sharp barbs. The whole episode reminded him of life in Third World countries – create chaos and then take advantage of it. The protestors just didn't realize that chaos was a cousin of conspiracy — it rarely had the intended effect. And as for Norm: Before that night he didn't even like fish.

At that moment Ray decided to enter the restaurant. He saw Norm and joined him in the booth.

"Have they finished carving up the free world?" Norm asked.

Ray waved at the waitress.

"Might as well save yourself the effort. She won't serve our kind," Norm brought Ray up to speed. He couldn't have been more surprised when she raced over with a piece of apple pie and a cup of coffee.

"I'm a regular," Ray explained.

"Must be the uniform," Norm mumbled.

"They carve me up in there?" He nodded toward City Hall and where he thought the meeting room was located.

"Don't flatter yourself." Ray sank his fork into his pie.

"They didn't ignore me, did they? Nothing I hate more than being ignored."

"That sounds about right."

Norm frowned. He was distantly related to Ray. Norm had agreed to not tell anyone if Ray would do the same. It wasn't that Norm was ashamed of Ray. Even though Ray worked for the man, and had even tried to ticket Norm once for fishing out of season, he was family and you put up with family, even while disregarding most of what they had to say. It didn't bother Norm a bit that Ray could get served at the Lumber Baron while he was still waiting for a glass of water.

"A cup of coffee would sure taste good about now," Norm muttered. Ray apparently didn't hear him and shoved the last of his pie in his mouth, washing it down with coffee.

"We've known each other a long time," Ray told Norm. Norm winced. That was the usual opening line for either a loan or a blind date with someone's sister.

"I've still got the scar from that time I tried to cite you," Ray went on. "I don't hide the fact that I've never much liked you. I always thought of you as a loser-shit-disturber." Norm made a move to stand up. That was usually the first step toward sculpting another scar. "Sit down. The truth is, I never thought much better of myself either."

Norm sensed this conversation was going somewhere interesting. He sat down.

"I know what they say about me on the Rez'. I'm a sellout, and that's when they're being nice about it. I can live with that," Ray began again. "Now I find out that with this railroad blockade thing you actually know what you're doing. You know how I know? Because those guys in there at that meeting, they were frustrated as hell, or they're pissed off or just don't have a clue what to do next. That's respect and that's something I want a piece of. You got them listening to you. That's more than they ever did for me."

Norm became aware his mouth was hanging open, and he closed it.

"I'm not looking for praise or thanks or anything like that," Ray explained. “The truth is, I’m ashamed I had to hear it from a white guy with a weird hat to convince me. So, what I’m saying is, go do what you gotta do, and I’ll do what I can to help cover your back.”

They shook hands silently before Ray left.

Now, watching the patrons of the Lumber Baron eating things southern fried or smothered in gravy, topped with a choice of pies, Norm didn’t feel the same anger he did when he walked into this place twenty years ago. The people here — the angry customers, the angry waitresses, the angry cook — didn’t realize they lived under the same thumb as the tribes. There were more similarities than differences. They had common enemies: the multi-national corporations, the power brokers, the arms merchants. The American people had more in common with the Panamanians than the Kuwaitis.

The biggest difference was that the tribes were awakening to the truth. But with an emerging Ojibwe middle class, places like this one were cutting their own economic throats. It would be a museum someday.

He removed a cigarette from his pocket and unpeeled the paper. He gathered the loose tobacco and placed it behind a sugar dispenser where it could make it through the rest of the day unseen.

He wanted to induce a spirit to come and collect the offering. It would be good for a laugh and even the spirits need a good laugh once in awhile.

IV. Intimate Fears

Angeline moved slowly at work the next morning, her legs feeling heavy and her head hurting. She didn't think about leaving the Island anymore, but mostly because it would require more emotion than she was ready to feel today.

Then she heard Lenny's bike tires squeal on the sidewalk outside The Restaurant where she stood inside with her order pad and pen poised, ready to record a relatively exotic food order for an older couple from Calgary.

Lenny rushed in, out of breath as always.

"Have you heard? Ben's buying a boat."

There were incidents and then there were incidents.

"Damn!" she muttered. Leave it to Ben to promote a crisis when all she wanted was an easy day at work.

So, that's why she hadn't seen him all day, she thought. She'd hoped he'd found a healthy diversion, or a discarded men's magazine, not potential cataclysm. She did not exaggerate. True, Ben would pose a danger to himself out on the open water, but he'd pose a much greater danger to everyone else.

"Hold the fort," she said, turning to the other waitress on duty. "Someone has to talk him out of this."

She found Ben at the marina admiring his new boat. She noticed he was admiring it from the dock, not the deck.

If his restaurant was a Walk-in-Hell, then this boat was last used to carry the damned across the River Styx. It looked like some kind of small tugboat with car tires hung from the rails. That couldn't be a good sign. It had a wheelhouse amid ship and an honest-to-God protruding smokestack. It looked like something from a cartoon where animal characters can hit each other with big sticks and see little birdies fluttering above their heads.

"You haven't actually paid money for this already, have you?"

"You like it? Now, I don't have to wait for the ferry."

"But you're afraid of the water," she reminded him.

"I'm not going in the water. I'm going over the top of it. There's a difference."

"That's semantics."

"Law of physics. I'm not sure which one. Want to go for a ride?"

If she couldn't talk him out of it,

she reasoned, at least she could accompany him on the first trip to make certain he didn't kill himself.

"Let's go then," she said, climbing aboard. She understood politics. If you can't stop it, then pretend it was your idea from the beginning.

Ben managed to get the boat out of the marina hitting only two docks. Angeline thought it was an accomplishment when he missed all the other boats.

She relaxed her grip once they were out on the open water, though her knuckles turned white again when he decided to race across the ferry's bow.

Fortunately, the ferry captain recognized Ben for the amateur he was and changed course.

They wandered past the Island's western point and its lurking sandbar. As if suddenly remembering what the steering wheel was for, he turned right. When she asked him where they were, he shrugged, and pointed to a collection of charts above his head. She pulled one down, unrolled it, couldn't make sense of it, and put it back.

"We must've turned left at Hermit Island," she said to herself, knowing Ben really didn't care.

It was a trivia question locals asked the tourists: How did Hermit Island get its name? Everyone knew Hermit Island as if it had the best publicity agent of the chain. It was the Island of undisguised disappointment in love.

According to legend, the hermit, having amassed a fortune before the turn of the century, when a lot of white people were amassing fortunes in northern Wisconsin, decided to get a mail-order bride. To make sure she'd be happy here, he built a beautiful Victorian style "cottage" on Hermit Island. The house, however, wasn't enough to overcome the isolated landscape. She took one look at it and left, never to return. The house was left empty until it finally collapsed on itself.

Funny, Angeline thought, so many of the Western culture's legends were about love. The Ojibwe legends she knew were a cut above, she thought. They were about things like where the first man came from, how the Apostle Islands were formed, and how the beaver got his tail.

"What really happened with you in Chicago?" she asked.

"What do you mean?" he answered. She wasn't sure if he was practicing denial or if he'd been truthful from the outset.

"The whole story."

"You think I'm full of it?"

"Working for you, I've figured out that lawyers don't lie. They just don't tell the whole truth," she said, slicing his favorite bologna very thin.

"Everything I tell people is true. I was in the civil rights movement. I didn't just meet Martin Luther King, Jr., I strategized with him. Get it? Strategized?" he insisted.

"The whole truth ..." she repeated, equally insistent.

"God, I loved it. The eye of the storm. The right place at the right moment in history ..."

She stared at him, unblinking, saying nothing. He flinched.

"There is one lie. I tell people that the mob put out a contract on me and that's why I left Chicago, but that's not true. It just sounds better than, 'My wife gave me an ultimatum.' She said, 'We leave Chicago or I leave Chicago.' So, we left Chicago, moved up here, bought the restaurant."

"Ben, you're a romantic. I'd have never guessed."

"Not me. Not then. I was the idealist. My wife was the romantic. You'd think those two would be a good mix," he said, then shook his head side-to-side. "Both are dreamers, both passionate about what they believe in. But it didn't work. She didn't like it up here and moved back to Chicago with the kids. Turns out it wasn't Chicago she hated, so much, as Chicago with me in it."

“Why’d you stay?”

“Out of spite, at first. Then, it was like we had switched roles and I became the romantic. I liked it. I wouldn’t have left Chicago in the first place if I hadn’t lost faith. You know how I knew?”

“No clue.”

“Disco … all that sacrifice and hard work, laying it on the line. I figured Utopia was just around the corner. But disco? It didn’t look anything like Utopia to me.”

Ben glanced at his watch and turned around, back into the North Channel between Hermit and Madeline islands, pulling Angeline from her self-absorption with a hand on her shoulder, then pointing off the starboard side at something in the water. She couldn’t see whatever it was he saw. Most of the time that was reassuring.

He turned in that direction, heading directly toward Madeline Island. First the wake appeared, then the head. As they got closer she could see a bear swimming in the water. It wasn’t an easy swim in waters two hundred feet deep. Ben throttled back and paced the bear for awhile.

"I've heard of bears swimming between the islands, but never saw one before," he said to Angeline.

If this was a legend in Angeline's life, it would be called, "How the Bear Learned to Swim by Trying to Stay the Hell Out of Ben's Way." She thought the bear tried looking back to make eye contact with her. Nothing else was on the water, not even a fishing boat. Nothing moved on the surrounding islands.

"That's gonna change the whole balance of things," she intoned.

"If there was any to begin with."

Though it was late when the boat chugged into the marina, the sun was still up. The summer solstice — It would be light until after midnight with a faint glow holding on in the northwest well beyond that time.

"That was ..." Ben struggled to find the word, 'fun' wasn't in his vocabulary. Most other adjectives had been stretched out of shape by the connotations that made up his life. "... good."

Angeline helped him tie the boat to the dock after he ricocheted off a pier and an adjoining boat.

"You surprised me," she admitted.

"Not that I want to make a habit out of confronting fears," he confessed. "But the truth is, when you got here this morning, I'd just about made up my mind I was never stepping on board this boat — ever."

"What's next? Bungee jumping?" she asked as they walked the long docks back to the shore.

"Maybe I'll try listening to my kids. It's been a few years," he answered, choosing an even larger fear.

She left him sauntering toward the bar, exercising his right to brag about the excursion to others who'd already drunk too much.

V. Panama North

The National Guard Armory in northern Wisconsin was a spare brick building, more Spartan in appearance than most dry cleaning outlets, with fewer whistles and bells than a monastery. This particular armory housed an engineering unit and had a parking lot crowded with bulldozers and front-end loaders, with the occasional Humvee – the envy of suburbanites with disposable income. This particular National Guard unit was not known for its warfare prowess, but for the miles of road it had constructed in its storied history, its personnel recruited from the best county road construction crews in the northern tier of Wisconsin. It was a crack unit when it came to knocking down trees and laying gravel. Warfare, whether that involved traditional ideological enemies, or competing multi-national corporations, was not its forte.

Inside the stark building a weekend colonel sat behind his army surplus desk in a small room with no windows. His paper shuffling was interrupted by the entrance of a young weekend lieutenant who didn't bother to salute before filling a cup of coffee and finding a comfortable chair.

"Lieutenant, we have a situation out on the reservation – civil disobedience breaking out all over," the colonel began, lifting his feet to rest them on top of the desk. "The governor has ordered the National Guard in to help restore order."

The lieutenant, who was in the act of lifting his coffee cup to his lips, paused in mid-lift. This didn't sound like a road-building project to him. This sounded like a real police action.

"We have some heavy armor on its way up from Madison. Personnel trained in riot control, but they want someone local, someone who knows the terrain, who knows the roads so to speak, to lead the mission. That's why I recommended you," the colonel continued.

"I'm honored," the lieutenant said, then thought the gravity of the situation compelled him to add the word, "sir."

"The thinking is that the presence

of National Guard personnel alone might be enough to restore order. That's the mission, to establish a presence, nothing more. Do you understand?"

The lieutenant nodded in the affirmative.

"I have to ask colonel, what if we're fired on?"

"I think that's unlikely, however, we do have reports that there might be guns in the camp. You have the right to defend yourselves, but take no aggressive action unless you're fired on first. These people are calling themselves peaceful protestors, so I don't expect violence, but be prepared."

"Yes ... sir," the lieutenant answered, wishing there was a window in the room he could look out. "I can't help wondering though, you say they're peaceful protestors. What happens if they throw themselves in front of the tanks, like that Tianaman Square deal in China?"

"You are not to squash any protestors. I want that understood. You are not to squash anyone! Do you understand!?" the colonel said with his jaw set and his eyebrows furrowed. It was the same expression he had used when he'd informed his troops, while on a road building training exercise in Panama the previous year, that they were to use condoms when fraternizing with the locals.

"Yes, sir."

"You leave tomorrow. We'll brief everyone when you muster in the morning. Dismissed."

VI. Moving Day

It was Angeline's day off and, despite previous experience she had with making plans in her life, she planned to take the time and do what she wanted to do — draw. Perhaps she would continue her engine-rebuilding series, or try some life drawing at the nude beach on the north end. She'd mull over that decision by paying someone else to make breakfast for her. However, as she drove through town, the unexpected sight of a recent acquaintance, carrying two suitcases, walking into The Island Hotel, altered her plans dramatically. He looked as angry as he did the last time she'd seen him, except this time she saw him without the house, without the Dobermans, and without the racial slurs. Overcome with curiosity, she had to find out what was going on.

She drove up to the north end, parked her Suzuki behind Orchid's Chevrolet and waved at Orchid's mother in the back seat as she walked past, heading down the path to the beach.

Angeline almost laughed out loud when she saw Orchid hunkered down behind a clump of bushes, peering through the branches at the house. Orchid turned, and motioned with her hand for Angeline to come and take a look.

"Where?" Angeline whispered.

Orchid pointed.

"Watch the back porch."

Angeline did exactly that. Within a few moments she saw the cause of all the chaos. A bear crawled out from under the porch, snuffled around a bit, found one of the dog's chew toys, and carried it with him back under the porch. He looked somewhat bedraggled, as if his had been a long and arduous journey to reach this juncture, underscoring the importance of this mission.

"He's moved in," Orchid explained. "Funny thing, too. Because he's a sacred animal, he can't be removed without the tribe's permission. It's the law."

They both fought to hold back the laughter, walking away from the beach to their parked cars, and when they thought they were a safe distance away, let it all burst out. They laughed so much they fell down on the ground, holding their stomachs and kicking their legs.

VII. Bad Information

It was a sound Norm hadn't heard in fifteen years, but once you've been there, you never forget. It was armor. There was no question. It was armor.

Norm and a friend had been walking the back roads around the protest camp, pretending that they were gathering more firewood, while spending most of their time smoking cigarettes and talking. That's when they heard the distinctive sound of heavy equipment being moved on metal tracks instead of rubber wheels.

"What the hell – "

An armored personnel carrier broke through the underbrush, trying to stay on a dirt road that had been designed for much less imposing vehicles. Norm, wearing his trademark army fatigue jacket, stepped into the roadway to be seen better, relatively confident that the driver would see him before crushing him under the weight of this motorized castle, or failing that, Norm guessed he was still nimble enough to get out of the way. It turned out to be the first option. The armored personnel carrier came to a grinding halt, a truck stopping behind it, and a Humvee behind the truck wound down its engine. The convoy sat, engines idling as a young man in full combat gear approached the two protestors.

“I wonder if you could help us,” the young army lieutenant said. “Army National Guard. We’re looking for the riot. We’ve been called in for riot control.”

“Impressive,” Norm said, looking over their equipment. “I haven’t seen anything like that since Panama.”

The army man puffed up his chest, taking obvious pride in his equipment. “You’re ex-army, then?”

“Regular army, attached to Special Forces in Panama and other locations in Central America,” Norm introduced himself, extending his hand.

“Real army,” the lieutenant remarked, obviously impressed. “I bet you got to see the world.”

“More of it than I expected,” Norm answered. “What are you weekend warriors doing out here on a beautiful day like this?”

“Riot control. We’re here to restore order.”

“You got some bad information.

There's no riot here, just a peaceful protest," Norm explained.

"You say, no rioting? You sure?"

"Positive. I did my share of riot control. Know one when I see one," Norm said. "FUBAR."

"FUBAR. Excuse me. I got to check in."

The army man returned to his vehicle.

"FUBAR? Is that Ojibwe?"

"Army talk. You don't want to know."

Norm and his friend listened in to the army man's half of the conversation.

"That's right, sir. There's no apparent riot anywhere that we can see. Looks like we got some bad information."

They could hear a high-static reply, too garbled to understand.

"That's right, sir. Bad information." After an appropriate

staticky response, the lieutenant responded. “That’s my assessment of the situation, sir. I have good reason to trust my source.” There was more static before the lieutenant hung up his mouthpiece. He then returned to speak with Norm.

“I want to thank you for your analysis of the situation, sir,” he said to Norm. “We’ll be heading back now. Can I get your help directing traffic? It’s not easy turning this monster around.” The lieutenant then looked around at the surrounding trees and shrubs, as if he making one last assessment. “You know, we could widen this road for you. It wouldn’t take much. Maybe even lay down a little gravel, too.”

“I appreciate the offer,” Norm said. “But this road isn’t used much anymore. I’m sure you guys have more important roads to build.”

“Let me know if you change your mind. In the meantime, we could use some direction turning these beasts around.”

“I know the drill. Happy to be of

service." As the army man prepared to come about, Norm to turned to his buddy. "I never thought army training would ever be any good to me or anyone else."

VIII. Forced Hand

The sheriff had given it a lot of thought and it still looked like there was no choice. It was obvious now. If he didn't, someone else would and then things could get way out of hand.

It became obvious when that railroad problem-solver had come down to the sheriff's office for a visit. Just a visit he said. He seemed friendly. He pretended he was in charge. Kind of an egomaniac and the sheriff had experience with egomaniacs, former bosses coming to mind.

Netherton kept pushing for the Sheriff's Department to do something. Those protesters were breaking the law.

"Strictly speaking," the sheriff answered, "That's federal law."

But everyone knew the feds wouldn't do anything about it. Sure, they drove around in their black SUVs and hovered in their helicopters, but they wouldn't do anything. Ever since Waco …

But that's not what bothered the sheriff. It was something Netherton had said on his way out the door.

"You know," he said, like he was talking to some buddies of his in an exclusive fraternity, "If you look the other way I can make your problem go away."

Rumor had it there were tribal men in the woods surrounding the camp, men with deer rifles and scopes, some of them with the best training the U.S. Army had to offer.

If it was true, things could get out of hand real fast.

The sheriff had to do something, if only to prevent others from doing it first.

IX. Connections

"This is nice," Angeline said, once the laughter had subsided and a cool breeze greeted her and Orchid where they lay on the ground along the trail on the Island's north end.

"People don't get close enough to the earth anymore," Orchid said. "They think because their feet touch the ground, that's good enough. But when you stand up, your heart is still a long way from the earth. This is better."

"So, tell me how you did that," Angeline said, rolling over onto her stomach. "You must have some really good connections."

"It wasn't me. Well, it wasn't me any more than it was you. It is connections, but not the kind you think. It's all connected," Orchid answered. "Now is a time when things are coming home. You came home. Maybe other things will, too."

"Why does he want to go to the reservation?"

"The spirit stones were used to guard the entrances to the Midaewin Lodge, the healing lodge. This particular stone used to guard the east entrance, the entrance of the rising sun. That's his job. When the tribe was moved off the Island and onto the reservations, many things were lost. Now he wants to return to his people and that would be on the reservation."

There was an easy silence between the two women. Unlike some bad dates Angeline had experienced, when she felt she had to say something, and keep saying something or the worst could happen, like being rejected or, in some cases, not being rejected. Instead, the thoughts flowed in the way she trusted they were supposed to.

"What happened to all the bones? The ones they dug up on the Island?" she wanted to know.

"The Smithsonian, mostly," Orchid answered. "I've seen them. They have them in big boxes with signs saying where they came from: 'Madeline Island, Bad River, Red Cliff, Lac Courte

Oreilles, Lac du Flambeau, Mole Lake ...'"

"What's to stop anyone from bringing them back?"

"It's not that easy. You can't change one thing without changing everything attached to it," Orchid tried to explain.

"What's to stop us from driving down to the museum right now and just taking the Spirit Stone back to the reservation?" she asked.

"You can't just throw him in the back of a pick-up and drive home. There's ceremonies that have to be observed. You need powerful medicine men and the time has to be right. More than anything, the time has to be right. Besides, he's gotten heavier, not lighter, the same way we all feel when we carry a heavy load, when we're depressed."

"How do we know when the time is right?"

"You know. Sometimes it comes to you in dreams, sometimes in signs.

But you know. The spirits will tell you, they tell you what your part is and when they do, you do it right away. If you get impatient, if you try to do it all by yourself, it affects everyone. It changes things for you, for me, for everybody. You have to trust."

"I just knew it wouldn't be easy."

X. Settling Accounts

The mining company CEO sat at his desk in his corner office in the big glass building in Toronto. He was looking over computer print-outs, listening to a self-improvement tape from one workshop or another, this particular tape telling him that if he wasn't selfish, no one could be selfish for him. The door to his office opened and in strode a familiar idea man, vice-president-of-something-important. The idea man went straight to the chief's desk. The CEO turned off the tape. The idea man reached into his pocket and peeled off ten one-dollar Canadian bills, laying them on the desk.

"How did you know?" the idea man asked.

"I didn't. You did and then you told me, when you said they actually seemed to believe in what they were doing."

The idea man frowned, turned and left the office.

XI. Spirit Joke

An Ashland Police Department squad car moved slowly through a back alley behind the city's main street. Headlights illuminated the passageway crowded with garbage cans, empty crates and shipping pallets. A spotlight on the squad car flashed from one back door to the next.

The police officer yawned. It was his first week back on the night shift and he wasn't used to the hours yet. The routine nature of checking back doors didn't help. He turned off his car's air conditioner and rolled down the window, hoping the fresh air would wake him.

When he reached the Lumber Baron Cafe at the end of the alley, he stopped. He thought he heard a voice — shouting. He climbed out of the squad car, walked up to the door, and leaned close.

It wasn't shouting. It was laughter: loud, uproarious, and self-absorbed laughter.

He pulled on the doorknob. The door swung open.

Everything appeared as it should be inside. Armed with his flashlight, he searched the building, front and back. Nothing. The only thing that appeared out of place was a sugar dispenser sitting in the middle of a tabletop in a booth near the front window, not flat against the wall like all the others. A few grains of tobacco sat on the table near it.

XII. Movement

When the museum curator arrived in the morning to open the museum, he was amazed at how high the sun already hung in the sky. A person could cover a lot of ground on a day like this, he told himself. He took a deep breath and limped onto the museum grounds. Something in the yard caught his eye. He stepped near for a closer look.

The stone had moved again. He was sure of it. This time the scarred ground, bare from lack of sunlight, exposed the full rectangle where the stone had once stood.

"I'll have to keep an eye on you," he told the stone and didn't think it out of place addressing the stone as if it were alive.

XIII. The Showdown

It was a hot, humid day. The sacred fire was still burning, as it had throughout the blockade and seemed to be adding heat to the situation, the humidity holding the smoke low in the air.

In the late morning, Hutch sat near the fire on a log end eating his lunch. He was tired and hadn't had a shower in nearly three weeks.

In the beginning, it had been exhilarating, full of a sense of purpose and energy. Now … now, he felt the weight of it. He had to rein in his feelings and be responsible. He hated that.

Today, there would be more of the same.

He knew they were coming. They had sentries posted and twelve sheriff's deputies couldn't just sneak up without somebody noticing.

They walked down the dusty road toward the camp in a defensive formation. When they reached the open ground, they spread out in a line. They were armed to the teeth … as armed as the county budget allowed and since the taxpayer's revolt in the 1970s that wasn't much. Hell, Hutch knew that on weekends they didn't even have a car out on patrol between midnight and 8 a.m. It was a cost-saving measure. But somewhere they found the money to dismantle blockades.

Here were twelve deputies all in a line advancing toward the camp. It must have been every deputy they had, including the part-timers they only used once a year to watch the gate at the county fair.

The sheriff was out in front, the one who drank too much, the undersheriff next to him, the one who was better than most undersheriffs in the past. They were nearing the sacred fire.

Hutch thought about the vision in the sweat lodge months before. He'd seen a train pulling tanker cars. As the train reached the bridge over the Bad River the train derailed, falling into the river, a white powder streaming from the tankers into the river. Death and sickness followed — dead fish, dead animals, dead plants and sick and dying Anishinabe. Of course, at the time he didn't know what the white powder was. He didn't know until the story in the newspaper a couple months later, an announcement from the Environmental Protection Agency, that the railroad had applied for a permit to move powdered sulfide along these very tracks, across the Reservation, across the Bad River and across the Bad River Railroad Bridge.

It was strange, he thought, the way information arrives. You think it comes in a straight line but sometimes, rarely, the wisdom comes first, or, it was always there.

"Stop!" Hutch had called it out in a loud clear voice, although it seemed to him the voice of some ancestor who knew how to throw an authoritative voice. "Don't go past the line of that fire."

The sheriff stopped and, with him, all the deputies.

Hutch knew something needed to be done, but he wasn't sure just what yet. He understood the situation. Each one of those deputies probably had crosshairs on them already. Hutch knew they were out there in the woods, just in case. He hadn't encouraged them, but he hadn't objected either. But, here, in this moment, that was a problem. There was no line of communication, no chain of command. If he wanted to call them off, he couldn't. Hutch felt the sweat running down his chest and back. He saw the sweat forming on the chests and armpits of the sheriff and his deputies. Well, this was the reason the undersheriff had worked so hard fostering good relations with the tribe. Let's see if that had been worth it, he thought.

Hutch stood and walked over to the undersheriff. Brewster followed, standing behind Hutch, literally covering his back.

"Hutch," the undersheriff greeted him. "You're here illegally and the railroad wants to press charges."

"Here's the problem," Hutch said. "There's men in the woods with guns trained on you and I'm not sure I can control them. I'm telling you this for your own good."

The undersheriff looked around into the distant woods that surrounded them. He paused. His eyebrows furrowed. He looked at the sheriff. The sheriff caught the look and acted decisively.

"OK," the sheriff said, then continued in a loud voice as if speaking to unseen warriors in the woods, or the ancestors who surely must have gathered by then. “We came to check it out and see if there were any problems down here. I don’t see any problems. We’re leaving.”

With that he turned and starting walking away, the deputies following.

Hutch watched them go, finally breathed, and went back to his lunch.

XIV. Testing the Theory

The various deputies dispersed once they were out of the camp and back to their vehicles, marked and unmarked, on the road. The sheriff had come in his own ride, rushing to meet the crew straight from his office where he had been laboring over paperwork. Nothing like a distasteful task you don’t even want to do to inspire you to throw yourself into paperwork.

He pulled open the door on his cruiser and climbed in, then sat down heavily behind the wheel. Nobody was going to be happy with his decision – not the railroad, not the DA, not the state and not the feds. But he felt pretty good about it.

He did what he said he would do – went down to the site and looked around. The rest was a judgment call. Yeah, discretion said you don't challenge unseen gunmen in the woods. But when he said he didn't see any problems, he meant it. Truth is, he could see it from the Ogichidaa point of view. As for the railroad and the feds, they'd have to find a way to solve their own problems.

At least this way he'd find out if the old man, had been right – that a county sheriff is the most powerful job in Wisconsin.

Chapter Ten

I. Golf Coach

From behind a large pine tree at the edge of the miniature golf course, Equilibrium peeked out to see if the coast was clear. It was, so she crept up to the eighteenth hole, carrying her soiled shopping bag with her. There, she knelt down, once again looking in both directions, then pulled a small box from the bag, the kind of box that had once held some kind of popular snack of the empty calorie variety, now painted to look like a glass office building, and placed it on the artificial turf. Next, she removed a toy airplane from the bag. Starting from the railroad blockade, she manually flew the plane to the office building and safely landed it.

"Hey!"

She turned to look. The local miniature golf pro stood nearby, shaking his fist at her. "What do you think you're doing?"

She jumped up and ran, almost forgetting her shopping bag.

II. An Invitation

A lone Sheriff's Department squad car arrived the next morning at the protest camp just as the sun was starting to warm the air, but before it became outright hot. Norm watched it arrive with interest. He had walked to the end of the road that connected the blockade camp with the nearest gravel road. He needed to get away, if only for a few minutes. The tracks could be blockaded without him for a while. He needed a smoke. It was a bad habit, one he had picked up in AA. If you didn't smoke before you started attending meetings you would before long.

He watched the undersheriff climb out of his car. Norm knew it wasn't bad news. The morning usually meant serving summons, delivering messages, taking statements – routine stuff. Felony arrests, or tragic news could happen anytime, but didn't usually. Interventions into potentially hazardous blockades almost always happened later in the day.

As the driver's door on the squad car opened, the undersheriff climbed out.

He glanced around a bit, saw Norm and headed in his direction.

"Good morning, Norm. Mind if I talk with you for a minute?"

"You're the one who's on the clock," Norm answered.

"The folks from the mining company want to talk to you. They asked me to give you this, I suppose because they don't exactly feel comfortable coming into the camp," he said, handing Norm an envelope. "I told them I'd give it to you, but I wasn't gonna try to convince you one way or the other."

Norm tore the envelope open. Inside, he found a plane ticket to Toronto and a hotel room confirmation.

"They want to talk," the undersheriff said.

"Why me?"

"You can send anyone you want. But Hutch probably won't leave and at least you know the score," the undersheriff explained.

There was a brief note, basically listing the itinerary with the time of a scheduled meeting with the company CEO and advisors and a plane ticket.

"Cheap bastards," Norm muttered. "It's coach."

III. Laundry Day

If there were two kinds of people in the world – those who do the laundry every week, faithfully, and those who let it pile up – Angeline was the kind who let it pile up. It was a metaphor of her life. She let things pile up until the load was too heavy to carry any further.

She threw all of her dirty clothes onto a blanket and tied the corners into a bundle, then rolled it to the Suzuki. She was barely able to lift it, in part because it was so heavy, and mostly because she had to cram it into the only available space between all her junk.

That could be a metaphor, too, she thought. If her meager possessions symbolized the accumulated junk of her life, the pieces of her past she couldn't let go of, then she was running out of room to put it all.

She let gravity do the work once she reached the Laundromat, the bundle of laundry landing audibly on the ground. She rolled it across the parking lot, through the door and in front of the bulk washing machine, the one that promised it could handle six loads without strain.

She broke open the bundle and was struck in the face by the odor of accumulated human scent. She didn't mind so much. It was mostly her scent. She loaded the machine, fitting closer to seven loads in the washer, added detergent and quarters, and turned around.

“Oh!” She knew he was predisposed to surprise entrances but she’d have never expected to find him here. Once her heart settled down, she said, “I got to warn you, I didn’t put any coffee on.”

“I’ve started limiting myself to one cup a day,” he answered, pulling his hand-woven blanket closely around his shoulders.

Grandfather looked a little haggard, although she'd have never told him that. She'd never hear the end of it.

"I didn't know you did laundry."

"The rain and the wind take care of me. I wanted to congratulate you. Good diversion."

"Me? What diversion?"

"Oh, you know, the train and tracks and all of that. Good diversion."

"I didn't do that. I never do that."

"You do it all the time, you just don't know it. You can't help it."

Now that she thought about it, maybe she did. She couldn't always point to some kind of causal effect, but chaos followed her like the moon chases the sun.

"What's next?"

"Let it build," he said. "We need a lot of force. Take care of everything in one big blow," he said, extending his arms dramatically.

"If you're going to take care of everything, do you think you could do something about the miniature golf course, too?" she asked, unimpressed with his grand gestures.

"I'll see what I can do," he said, almost growling. "After all, you can't expect miracles."

"One more thing," she said, pushing her luck. "The other night I saw these two little men – "

"You saw Little People?" he asked, suddenly interested. "What did they tell you?"

"To run."

"Hmm. I should have warned you, but I never thought they would visit you. You have to do the opposite of what they say."

"Are they a bad thing, or something?" she wanted to know.

"No, no, not at all. It's good luck to see them. But they talk backwards, so you do the opposite of what they say."

It began to rain gently on the Island, what the locals called a squall — nothing more than a low-flying cloud that would pass quickly.

Grandfather took advantage of the opportunity, walking into the falling rain to do his laundry.

Angeline waited while her laundry passed through the wash cycle, occasionally looking up at a pay phone hanging on the wall. She still had coins in the coffee can where she deposited her tips. She could call home and hope she and her mother could avoid the same old emotional buttons. Angeline stood, walked over to the pay phone, lifted the receiver, briefly read the instructions printed on the face of the phone, thought about what she might say, then replaced the receiver. She wasn't ready. She could still feel the storm clouds gathering inside her. She just wasn't ready yet. Instead, she placed her clothes in the dryer and left to help a friend drop an engine back in her Jeep.

IV. High Level Conference

Norm tried looking up to the top of the glass building in Toronto. When he couldn't bring the peak into view without straining his neck he decided it wasn't worth it and stopped trying, walking inside through a revolving door.

After scanning the list of companies and their respective floors, he chose the express elevator — all the way to the top floor. That told him something about the health of mining companies these days. They weren't hurting, he told himself. They must be eating well and could probably afford luxury boxes for Toronto Bluejays baseball games, liberally distributed to preferred clients and sympathetic politicians. Norm had to talk himself out of being impressed, and then thought, "What the hell, it's impressive. I'll be impressed."

The elevator ride left his stomach catching up with his body. It reminded him of a helicopter on a short take-off. It was a sensation he usually tried to avoid.

The receptionist recognized him immediately, one of the advantages of being Ojibwe in a corporate world. True, corporations hired the occasional aborigine, but Norm was wearing the ex-army uniform, fatigue jacket and a "They already did it to me" attitude, instead of the corporate three-pieces-and-a-power-tie uniform. The receptionist led him to a conference room with floor-to-ceiling glass, an expansive table, a coffee setting and pastry tray. He helped himself.

He didn't have to wait long. The door swung open and three men in suits, in ascending order of importance entered the room. Norm focused on the last man in, the CEO, no doubt ... slightly more expensive clothes ... a little older ... the only one who looked directly at other people ...

"You must be Norm," he said, extending his hand. Norm took the hand, but didn't hold it long. In Norm's world of priorities, the coffee cup was more important. The four of them chose places to sit around the massive table, the three corporate executives clustered around one end and Norm at the other. Norm knew all about superior numbers.

"This is about the impasse –"

"Let's be a little less formal," the CEO said, interrupting his assistant. "I'm Charles, named after a stuffy ancestor, I'm afraid."

"I'm named after an uncle who was killed in the war — World War II. He came back alive, but his spirit was mostly dead. He's been drinking himself to death since then," Norm responded.

"I appreciate your candor," Charles said.

"Shouldn't we discuss – "

Charles stopped his aide with a look. "Why don't you two leave us alone. I think we can handle this."

The two assistants, vice-presidents-of-something-important, looked at each other and grudgingly stood, then walked out.

"You'll have to forgive them. They take themselves too seriously at times," Charles apologized. "Don't misunderstand. They're going to do what they're going to do. That's the way of it with corporations. Put some ambitious young executives in charge and hope they want a promotion badly enough to make it happen. Corporations really do have a life of their own. Even I can't change that. How's the coffee. I had to give it up for health reasons."

"It's better than most. No after-bite, not yet anyway," Norm answered, sipping. He looked up and noticed Charles licking his lips. "I'll give you regular updates."

Charles laughed politely. "I understand you were in Panama?"

"We'd have to tip a few beers first to talk about that," Norm said. "Shouldn't we be talking about trains and sulfide and things like that?"

"Oh, I can't think why. Those matters usually sort themselves out. Tell me, what was it like for you growing up?"

"Eleven kids in the same house. My parents loved each other as long as they could, until their lives beat them up too much and they couldn't love anybody anymore, especially themselves.

Of the people I've cared about in my life, most of them gave up in some way long before they died, and more of them are dead than alive."

"How sad. Are both of your parents gone?"

"Both of them, although half of my brothers and sisters died first. That's the usual."

"I can't imagine anything worse for a mother than to outlive her children," Charles sympathized. Norm was momentarily confused by Charles' negotiating strategy. Then he recognized a familiar method, one used repeatedly through the centuries. This time, however, instead of buying him a train ticket to Washington, D.C., and turning his head with big stone buildings, and men in suits and beaver skin hats, they flew him to Toronto and were plying him with admittedly good coffee. He would be wary if they tried to give him yellow army blankets.

"How's the coffee now? You promised me regular updates."

"Still no after-bite," Norm said.

Charles stood and walked to the floor-to-ceiling windows, looking out on the city. Norm stayed where he was, still getting over the elevator ride. Besides, windows like that, especially at this altitude, made him feel like he would spill over the edge. He left these kinds of heights to eagles.

"You've had a difficult life," Charles commented.

"I've had it easy. My parents, my grandparents, my great-grandparents, they had it hard."

"I, on the other hand, have had it easy. I've thought about that often, how the accident of birth affects our lives. I didn't get to be CEO of a major corporation and its interlocking boards because of any great skills on my part, or any strength of character, no more than anyone else who climbed the same ladder. I'll tell you what passes for hardship in my family, and it's ironic. Madeline Island plays a part in this drama. My ancestors were there once, almost three-hundred and fifty years ago.

They traded with the Ojibwe, put together a fortune in furs. But they didn't have permission from the French governor, so their cargo was confiscated. Because of that, they weren't able to return to France and had to amass their fortune the hard way. Part of that fortune was stock in this company that I inherited."

"I almost feel sorry for you," Norm said.

Charles smiled, an ironic smile, Norm thought, from what he could see. Then Charles turned back to Norm. "I like your sense of humor. Don't get me wrong. I'm trying to persuade you to drop the blockade. Yet there are many things I admire about what you're doing. I can't imagine people in my world acting so much in concert and so unselfishly."

"We're in concert, all that practice from planning funerals together," Norm answered, finishing his cup of coffee.

That must have struck some emotional string for Charles. His focus shifted onto something distant. That's when it struck Norm. Sure, Charles was trying to get his way. Stop the blockade, clear the tracks and make a profit, but he could have chosen a thousand different approaches. Instead, he was coming at it from an angle that allowed him a glimpse, maybe even a vicarious role in Norm's life. *He just wants to know what it's like to be me. He's lonely in his big glass house,* Norm thought.

Charles didn't have to bail his nephew out of jail every time he got arrested. He probably had someone on staff to do that, if he even had a nephew who got arrested. Instead of loaning money to friends, money he'd never see again, he could just arrange for a line of credit. He probably sent expensive bouquets to funerals, left early, and didn't have to stay up all night at the wakes. Norm wondered if Charles ever had to choose between visiting the friend in the hospital who was beat up by the nephew who went to jail for battery, or visit the nephew in jail who had threatened to hang himself the next time he was behind bars.

"So, what is this all about? Show the Indian the big glass house so he knows there's no hope? Or maybe it's the guilt thing. Sometimes there's no real difference between bigotry and sympathy," Norm began, almost as if thinking out loud.

"I'm sorry, I don't follow you," the CEO answered, still seeming to be on friendly terms but Norm could feel the walls going up. Inside, he felt his stomach muscles knotting up and it wasn't from the coffee.

"You have a strange fascination for hardship, like you don't get enough of it," Norm told him. "You look at my life and you admire it, because of all the reality. You put me on a pedestal. But I don't want to go there either. Yeah, I got a lot of reality in my life, more than I ever wanted. All I've ever tried to do is deal with it the best I could. But wait, maybe you want some Indian wisdom, wisdom that I had to pay a helluva price for."

"I'm listening," the CEO said, his jaws tightening. Norm leaned closer, dropping his voice almost to a whisper so Charles would have to work harder to hear him, Norm chewing the words before he let them out.

"Funny thing, my people never used to get cancer. We had a way of dealing with the hurt. Make a demon, ugly and angry. You yell at the demon some, feel better and he leaves to help someone else. But that was long before the railroads showed up on the scene. You asked about my family. Here's a story you can appreciate. One of my brothers used to live on a choice piece of land by the river. Flooded every spring and when the water went down, he'd tap the maple trees and make sugar. Lived for it. I'd help him out sometimes and he'd give me some of the syrup. Then, a few floods later, an old paper mill landfill opened up and spilled into his well. He lasted three years, but you could see it in his face. He was dying a little all the time. The last year he didn't make sugar at all. I haven't made any since."

Charles looked at Norm for several seconds, then looked down and away.

"I'm truly sorry," he said to the

glass window.

“Charlie? Can I call you Charlie?”

“Certainly.”

“Charlie, I sympathize with you in some ways. It couldn’t have been easy growing up being groomed to become king of the known mining world, preparing to lead a corporate giant when all you really wanted to do was play baseball until the sun went down. But that’s your role in life and I’m sure it has its compensation. As for me, my role was to get jerked around by life and caught in the middle every time the politicians and power brokers decided to stare each other down. My only compensation is that I get to hold the high moral ground. You can’t have that. It’s not in your role, Charlie. I have bad news for you. This time you have to play the demon. We’re gonna yell at you some, try and chase you away. It’s an important role, don’t get me wrong, but you don’t get to feel good about it. Win, lose or draw, that’s what I get and I’m not giving that up, too.”

On the flight home, Norm felt like an eagle flying over the Upper Peninsula, heading toward Duluth. This line of approach would take them over the reservation and Madeline Island when they were well into their final descent.

He thought about an Anishinabe story, warning really, his grandfather had told him when he was growing up. When Migizi the eagle flies over the world, and can no longer see the smoke from Anishinabe fires, that's when the world will end. Of course, they were flying too high to see a campfire from up here. It would have to be a forest fire, but he knew there was a fire burning at the camp by the tracks.

A stewardess approached him, interrupting his thoughts.

"We're starting our final approach, sir. Are you finished with your coffee?"

Norm looked at his cup, hardly touched.

"Yeah, this trip has spoiled me for bad coffee." He handed her the cup, put his tray in a locked, forward position, and looked out the window again. He thought he could see Madeline Island.

There were no Anishinabe living on the Island that he knew of. The master plan had worked. On the Island, the Anishinabe were so assimilated you couldn't find one. There weren't likely to be many in the future either, with land prices the way they were, especially lakeshore property.

Then he saw the railroad tracks heading toward the reservation. It looked like the toy tracks a friend of his had when they were kids, and there was a train down there, too, that looked like — Damn! he thought. It looked like a lot of tankers, the kind used for transporting chemicals, like sulfide. It didn't seem to be moving too fast, if at all, but it was there as big as a snake with an after-bite.

V. Restoring Power

Glenda had the Jeep''s engine poised, hanging from the block-and-tackle above the Jeep's open engine well. To Angeline, it looked like open-heart surgery.

"Almost ready?" Angeline called

out to her friend as she approached.

"Almost. You lower the block-and-tackle and I'll guide it in," Glenda instructed. Angeline took up her position and followed the instructions Glenda issued. When the engine was back in place, Glenda went to work, reattaching the various lifelines while Angeline handed her tools.

"So why couldn't I do it?" Angeline asked, referring to her aborted phone call home. "Why can't I bring myself to call her?"

"You've built a wall of some kind. Make no mistake, you're getting in your own way. What do you think it is? I need that crescent wrench over there."

Angeline picked up the wrench and handed it to Glenda.

"When I pick up the phone, I just feel myself getting tight, bracing myself for whatever controlling thing she's going to do next. Sometimes it's intentional sometimes it isn't, but it always hurts. Like when she asks me about my hair. I dye my hair black. My mother hates that. She thinks I do it to look more Indian and, of course, reject her. And to be honest, maybe that's why I do it, to look more Indian, but not to automatically reject her."

"Could you hand me that hose and clamp?" Glenda asked. Angeline did so, without even having to ask which was the hose and which was the clamp.

"It's the whole assimilation thing on a microcosmic scale. She wants me to just settle down and accept who I am. But in her mind, who I am means the Catholic daughter of suburban parents from German and Norwegian background, instead of the adopted daughter, raised in the Catholic church by German and Norwegian suburbanites, in conflict with her Indian heritage. That whole conflict part, she doesn't even want to go there. She doesn't want to see conflict at all. That was especially true when my dad was dying."

"I'll need that other hose and clamp, now."

"That whole time she was hiding out at the church, leaving me to take care of him," Angeline explained, handing the requested hose to Glenda. "One of the few illusions I had from my childhood was that my dad was this strong, normal, easy-going guy who loved me the best he could. Instead, I had to give him bed baths, empty his bedpan, and watch him wither away to nothing while my mom was at church praying for a miracle. She even turned that into some kind of test over whether her beliefs were stronger than mine."

Glenda crawled out from under the Jeep and began hooking up wires from above.

"Do you remember anything good from that time?"

"There was one thing. It was right after he told me that thing about God not being who my mother thought he was. That was when he told me to go and find out for myself, find out who I was," she answered.

"And now you're here."

"And now I'm here."

Glenda stepped away from the Jeep with a satisfied look on her face, mentally checking over the various connections one last time. Then she stepped around, climbed behind the wheel and turned the key. The engine groaned, sputtered, groaned and fired up. A smile beamed across her face.

"I couldn't have done it without ..." She looked around for someone to thank. Then it came to her. "...me."

Chapter Eleven

I. Lift

"So then when the railroad's big-shot negotiator from New Zealand got home and stepped off the plane, this big gust of wind grabbed his hat and threw it all the way into the ocean," Grandfather said as if it was the punch line to a joke. He laughed until he had to hold his stomach from the pain.

"You wouldn't know where that big gust of wind came from, would you?" Angeline asked with a touch of sarcasm as she and the old man sat by her fire that night.

She was in a foul mood. She was ready to sink some deep roots but felt like she was standing on a rock cliff. Grandfather didn't notice her mood at first and went on laughing. When he saw her furrowed brows he stopped and caught his breath.

"You did good. You did real good. Now what we need is lift. Lots of energy."

“How the hell am I supposed to do that? I don’t even know how I did the diversion thing,” she snapped.

“Confrontation, it always makes lots of energy,” he said, still smiling.

“...and what do you need all that lift for anyway?”

“To move a stone," he answered. The mischievous grin always caught something involuntary in her imagination.

“How high?”

“Oh, all the way to the spirit world and back again.”

“How far is that?”

“A long way, and then not so far.”

“Riddles ... I ask a civil question and I get riddles ...Why don’t we just go pick him up and haul him out of there?” She felt the blood rise from the pit of her stomach to her head. A sharp breeze blew through the camp scattering sparks from the campfire.

“He hasn’t told me to. Has he told you?”

“Me? Why me?” Distracted, she dropped her anger like an abusive boyfriend. The wind stopped and the air turned suddenly still. She looked up from the fire. Grandfather was smiling as if the answer to his question should be obvious to her.

“What other Anishinabe live on the Island?”

She looked away from him, the better to think. “I’ve got so many spirits talking to me these days I can’t keep them straight. Let me see ... there’s this crazy old man ... and a giant bear ... Little People ... but no, no stones.”

“He wouldn’t look that way in a dream, of course ...” he lead her in the direction of obvious answers.

She thought about it for a few moments. “Well, then, yeah, he’s been talking to me.”

“My advice is to keep listening.”

II. Almost Home

The night air was stagnant and moist. That meant a hot day to follow. Equilibrium felt safe when the world took on an unreal flavor. She crept back to the miniature golf course and knelt down by the stuffed bear, sitting down and cradling the bear in the crook of her arm.

"Do you know, we haven't been to the mainland in a long time. Would you like to go?"

She listened for his reply.

"Why can't you go yet?"

She held him up to her ear again, listening intently, her eyes growing wide.

"Oooooh ..."

III. Early Warning

The morning preparation in the Walk-in-Hell's kitchen quickly heated the restaurant, the patio outside and most of the immediate surrounding Island. If grandfather wanted energy, he could have some of this, Angeline thought as she removed fresh rolls from the oven, then wiped the sweat from her forehead.

She left the rolls to cool and made the rounds with a pot of hot coffee to freshen the cups for the morning breakfast crowd.

Glenda and Ursula, or maybe the other way around, were having morning coffee and nothing else.

“More coffee?” Angeline offered.

“Yes, dear,” Ursula answered. “Poor Glenda. She didn’t sleep well last night. She’s so intuitive. When the spirits are active, she doesn’t get a wink.”

“Something’s going to happen. I know it,” Glenda muttered, more to herself than anyone in particular.

Angeline sat down next to Ben, refreshing his coffee and pouring one for herself, sharing the newspaper and Ben’s second-hand smoke. The already warm air crackled with anticipation although the sun had been in full bloom for barely two hours.

“Disco, hunh?” she prompted a conversation.

“Disco killed it for a lot of people,” Ben answered, still reading.

“Tell me, Ben. When did you know you were an Islander?”

He put down the paper.

“The first time someone got seriously pissed off at me and I got pissed off right back,” he answered without hesitation.

Angeline looked up just in time to see the eagle land atop a telephone pole just across the street from The Restaurant. The look on her face must have been alarming. Ursula read her expression right away and followed her line of sight to the eagle.

“Oh, my!”

At which point Lenny burst into the room.

“There’s a train coming! There’s a train coming! There’s gonna be a confrontation!” he shouted and then disappeared.

Angeline placed the coffee pot on Ursula’s and Glenda’s table, pulling off her apron.

Angeline and Ben made immediate eye contact.

“I need a ride,” she told him.

“I have a boat.”

“Let’s go!”

IV. Hitching a Ride

Ben maneuvered the boat as close to shore as he safely could, fighting the waves to keep from running aground.

“This is the closest point to the camp, but there’s no dock. How do you feel about swimming?” he told her.

“How do you feel about swimming?” Angeline returned the question, scanning the remaining distance to shore.

“Me?”

"You're coming with me."

"You know how I am with water."

"Time to face those fears."

Without waiting, she peeled off her clothes, found a mostly empty garbage bag, stuffed her clothes inside. She held the bag open for Ben. Reluctantly, he followed suit, like a Democrat preparing for life under a Republican administration.

She dived head-first. Ben threw the bag in after her and did his version of a dive — feet first, holding his nose. Once he reappeared on the surface, he splashed noisily once and looked for all the world like he was going to flounder. Rather than point out his folly, she simply stood up, standing in about four feet of water. When his panic passed, he realized how foolish he looked and stood, too. Once again, she thought, the potential for embarrassment overcomes fear.

"You could have said something," he admonished her, wiping water from his face.

"You mean, like, 'Stand up, you big wuss?'"

"Something like that. It would have been the politically correct thing to do."

They dressed on the beach and walked to the nearest highway. Fortunately, several others had heard about the train and Angeline and Ben had their choice of rides to the camp. They chose one with towels.

V. Confrontation Eve

They arrived at the camp in time for a setting sun and a roaring campfire. A modest crowd sat around the fire listening to Norm tell about his adventure in Toronto.

"All I could think about was when I was in the army," he said. All eyes were on him, or staring vacantly into the fire. Angeline chose a stump end near the farthest reaches of light and watched Norm. Ben sat where it was warm and stared into the fire.

"In the army, in Panama, I saw a few examples of people doing what they really believed in, and it didn't do them much good. When you're talking the U.S. Army, or international corporations, they don't just walk away when there's a problem. They can lose a lot of battles and still win the war."

"What about Vietnam?" Jay asked. "The little guy won there."

"The one that got away, but the CIA learned from that one. The heavy hitters engage you, make you use up your resources until you're vulnerable, and then swoop in for the kill. And even if you win, they'll outlive you. Corporations never die, they just merge, absorb you, get bigger and change shape. And they never forget."

"And leave their mess behind for us to clean up," Brewster added the 'amen'. "I've seen what sulfuric acid can do. I learned it in chemistry class in the white man's school." He was getting on a roll, the way Brewster could. "You can't drink it. You can't put it on your plants. If it doesn't make the manomin grow, I say what good is it?"

A heavy silence hung over the camp. It felt like a weight, a pall. The fire didn't give off as much light. Even the stars seemed to be duller.

"I think about when Chief Buffalo rode the train to Washington, to try and talk the government out of removing us to Minnesota," Norm said. "They did that to discourage us — the long train ride, the big cities, millions of people. Just like flying to Toronto."

"They didn't try to buy you off, did they?" Jay asked.

"That's not the way it works. They don't have to try. Every time I turn on a TV, someone's trying to buy me off. Wear Nikes! Be like Mike! Drive a SUV! Drink Miller Lite! Accept your life! It's good. Assimilation ... The master plan is working. Look at Madeline Island. You can't find one Anishinabe on the Island, and there aren't likely to be any in the future with the price of lakeshore property."

"You're wrong!" All eyes turned

to Angeline, surprised. She surprised herself. “I’m Anishinabe and I live on the Island. I’m not going anywhere, no matter how high the price of lakeshore property goes.” Everyone looked back at Norm. He didn’t answer. He just stared at Angeline. She’d never seen his direct gaze before. His face was hard and his eyebrows furrowed. Decades of pain resided in that look. During the silence, his fists and jaws clenched. He looked like he was about to explode. But he just stood. Then, as if realizing for the first time that everyone was staring at him as if expecting an answer. Instead, he turned and walked away. So did nearly everyone else, each, in turn, shooting an angry look at Angeline, until she and Ben were the only ones left at the fire. Angeline felt like she’d committed the ultimate faux pas — she’d rained on a collective self-pity.

“You don’t have to stay,” she told him. “You have a business to run.”

“I have to stay, for a lot of reasons,” he answered, stretching out beside the fire seemingly immune to the moment’s tension. “Besides, my boat’s probably at the bottom of the lake by now."

"What did I do wrong?"

"You did two things wrong, not just one," he corrected her. "First, you spoke the truth in the face of sweet illusions. What a rude awakening. They'd almost talked themselves into giving up and then you slap them all in the face with the truth." He stopped talking just long enough to yawn, long, deep and self-satisfying. "Damn. I haven't yawned like that in ages. They say when you're getting old the first thing to go is ... well, you know. But the first things to go are the satisfying involuntary responses."

"What's the second thing I did wrong?" she got him back on track.

"When you realized, too late, that the mood was all gloom and doom, you shifted direction like your whole life is about making the social registry."

"What do you mean?"

"Look at yourself. You're feeling

sorry for yourself better than they ever did in their lives, and I'm the only one here to see it. Hey, it's wasted on me. Sweet dreams." He rolled onto his side, adopted a fetal position, and fell asleep.

VI. Sweet Dream

Angeline found a dry piece of ground to lie on and stared at the fire as long as she could keep her eyes open. Ben's feedback didn't help her mood. She felt more depressed than ever. She lost track of time and place and didn't remember closing her eyes and drifting off to sleep. Before long she heard snuffling sounds around her face and when she opened her eyes she saw the bear from close range. This time, however, she wasn't afraid. She had come to anticipate his visits and losing the element of surprise took some of the edge off. On this particular visit, she couldn't help but notice his forlorn mood. That told her something, too, that she was becoming adept at reading bear body language.

"What's up with you?"

“I want to go home,” he said, sitting down on his haunches. His head hung low and his shoulders slumped.

“Where’s home for you?”

“The reservation, with my people. I want to see the sun come up from my place at the eastern door of the lodge,” he told her.

“At least you know where home is,” she told him. She wanted to tell him that times had changed. Even if he went home it wouldn't be the same.

Instead of Anishinabe in traditional outfits, revering the stone that guarded the eastern door, revering the rising sun, he’d have to compete for attention with the Nike Swoosh and Super Bowl Sunday, the Star Wars action figures, the World Wide Web, and T-shirts whose only identifiable features were the designer’s name splashed across the front. Almost no one saw the sun come up in the morning anymore and if they did it meant they were 24/7 into a middle management job. Science had vanquished most diseases, most superstition, and with it, most reasons to rely on belief systems. It was the grand illusion of our times, she thought. In a world still pulsating with the magic of nature, and its many spirits, most people had insulated themselves from it in ways that slowly destroyed that fabric. While Angeline didn't know where home was, the Spirit Stone knew only a home that didn't exist anymore.

"I want to go home," he repeated.

"How?" she wondered.

He breathed deeply, then snorted outward, the resulting air gathering into a small whirlwind that engulfed him and carried him away like lowland mists carried away by the West wind.

"Oh..."

VII. Meeting of the Minds

After the bear's visit, Angeline drifted off for a few more moments of sleep. When she opened her eyes again she saw Hutch sitting on a stump-end near the fire. He was watching Angeline as if waiting for her to awaken.

“He come to you often?” Hutch asked.

He picked up a stick and stirred the coals in the fire, the tip of the stick spontaneously combusting.

“You saw him?” she asked, surprised that someone else shared her version of reality.

“No, but I felt his presence. Besides, you talk in your sleep.”

“I’ve seen him more often than I want, him and his buddies,” she answered, annoyance creeping into her tone of voice. Then she thought about the words she’d hurled at Norm earlier in the night. “I’m sorry about what I said. I didn't mean to make anyone look bad.”

“Sometimes that’s the only way to get anyone to listen, especially someone who thinks he knows it all,” he answered. He was trying to be forgiving, but it wasn’t easy for him. His jaws were tight as he spoke.

“He’s pissed off at me,” she speculated.

“He’ll get over it. It was probably something he needed to hear.”

“It was probably something I needed to do — piss someone off. In a strange way, I feel like I’m home,” she told him.

“Welcome home,” he told her, and smiled.

“I wish it was that easy. I thought, I’ll move to Madeline Island and feel like a real Indian. I still don’t know what that’s like,” she complained.

“What kind of real Indian? The real Indian from a thousand years ago before the white man showed up? I don’t know what that’s like either. I wear the outfit and on special occasions dance in the pow-wows, but it’s not the same. It’s good, don’t get me wrong, but it’s not the same. For my parents it was different than it is for me. For my nephews and nieces, it’s different. My parents went fishing because they needed it for food. There were no casinos and no jobs for them. I went fishing because the state said I couldn’t. Our children go on the Internet and talk with other Indians about going fishing."

"Maybe it's the hardship thing, you know, suffering together. I wasn't there for that. I haven't even got bragging rights about how bad it was for me."

"You didn't miss anything. Besides, I wonder what all that's worth anyway. After awhile it becomes a way of life. You know, like being pissed off for so long it becomes your natural state, so you end up like some middle-aged white guy who got downsized and divorced and can't see his own kids except when the court says so. How pathetic is that?"

She stared into the fire. She found that basic element soothing and reassuring.

"What's going to happen tomorrow?"

"I've been thinking about that all night. I feel like running and hiding. When a Indian runs, it's not to the reservation, or out into the woods. A Indian runs into the white world, into that overwhelming sea of white faces. You wear the clothes. You drive the car. You work the job.

That's what I did when I was young. I got lost in the assimilation."

He stirred the fire one more time and dropped another log on it. Norm, stretched out on the ground with his back to them, rolled over to face Angeline.

"That's what happened to me," Norm said. "But it doesn't work. No matter how white you try to be, sometime, somewhere, some way, someone will make it clear just how Indian you are. That's what happened to me. It was funny how it happened, too, stomping through the jungle in Central America. I got separated from my unit. I'm all in a panic, being chased by rebels, running here, running there.

"Then I bust through the underbrush right into this Indian village. They hide me. They feed me. They take my clothes and burn them and give me native clothes to wear. When the rebels came into the village looking for me, they didn't know me from any other Indian in the village."

"So, running's not an option."

"You can always run, but eventually you end up right where you started," Hutch said.

He held up his stick and watched the flame for awhile.

"I want to do this thing right. When the train comes, I don't want it to be just another glorious defeat. We have too many songs about those already. We're not just doing this to dump our anger and feel a little better for awhile. It has to change us and who we are, in a good way."

This time, when Angeline closed her eyes she was able to sleep undisturbed until she felt the sun on her face when it rose in the east.

VIII. Good Day for a Confrontation

Angeline heard sounds before seeing anything. First, a few pots and pans rattling against each other — a few spoons scraping against plates, a few subdued voices.

"You hungry?"

"Surprisingly, no," Angeline answered.

Then she heard the eagle screaming up above, and looked up. Two eagles were circling high above them.

"They've been there all morning," Hutch said, cooking fry bread over the fire. "Something's going to happen today."

The air was still and stagnant that morning and, after the early sunrise of a summer solstice, heat was collecting in the low places and refusing to leave. It was almost as if the perpetual fire in the camp had preheated the air. It could, with a short journey to the spirit world and back.

"How about you?" he directed the question at Ben.

"Like I've never been before," he said, sliding in beside Norm with a ravenous look on his face. He gratefully accepted a plate.

"You ever been through anything like this before?" Ben asked.

"Not when there weren't bullets flying," Norm answered.

"Kent State, huh?" Ben assumed.

He dug into the food as if he knew from some anarchist Bible that you ate when you could, as much as you could, as fast as you could.

One of the Ogichidaa walked up to Norm, leaned close and whispered in his ear. Norm walked away toward a nearby truck and took a cell phone from someone else. He talked for a while, handed the phone back and returned to the fire.

"That was a friend of mine, Ray," he told Hutch. "There's a train car on the way," he said.

Angeline looked back up at the sky. Hutch followed her line of sight. One of the eagles turned away and flew off into the distance, toward Madeline Island. The other circled on closer until it landed in a tall tree near the tracks, opposite the camp.

Immediately after, the TV cameras

arrived in a van sporting call letters and a satellite dish.

“This is it,” Hutch said. Angeline climbed to her feet and followed. Ben set aside his plate, and joined them still chewing on his food.

Hutch stood on the railroad tracks, standing inside the rails, while more Ogichidaa gathered at the tracks, surrounding Norm in a protective crescent. The confrontation began in a small way. Nothing was visible at first, but eventually a small, yellow, railroad inspection car came into view, its image distorted by radiant heat waves rising from the ground.

“That’s it? I'm not impressed,” Jay remarked.

“Don’t fall for it. There’s a full-blown train out there somewhere,” Hutch cautioned.

“The fear you can’t see is worse than the one you can,” Ben advised. “That way they use your imagination against you.”

The inspection car rolled to within

ten feet of the eagle lance and stopped, its engine idling.

"Let's make our move," Hutch said, approaching the inspection car, two warriors flanking him.

"Can I help you?" he asked the two men sitting inside.

"You'll have to clear the tracks. There's a train on its way," the driver, a clean-cut man in work clothes announced.

"We can't do that," Hutch responded, he looked at Brewster standing resolutely next to him.

The railroad man sat with a confused look on his face, as if his instructions had included the line: "Just tell them there's a train coming. They'll back down. They have to. What choice do they have?"

"I don't think you understand. There's a train behind me," he said again, looking back. There was nothing in sight.

"We understand. It makes no

difference. We're staying," Hutch restated.

The two men in the inspection car looked at each other and didn't respond.

They turned off the inspection car's idling engine as if to say they had nothing else to do but wait, and they were getting paid overtime to do it.

Hutch stood his ground. There was no reason to worry, as long as the lance was in place.

IX. Joined in Battle

The mining company CEO and his vice-presidents-of-something-important sat in the CEO's room-with-a-view, waiting. The room was completely silent, not a sound, not even a personal improvement workshop tape. Then the phone rang. The CEO gestured for a vice president to answer.

"Yes?"

There was a pause while the vice president listened.

"Very well, then. Keep us updated." He replaced the receiver.

“Our people are on the site. There’s still time for a bet ..."

The CEO was deep in thought. He looked up and shook his head, indicating he had lost his appetite for bets.

X. High Energy

The warriors ate their noon meal, careful to put out a spirit plate. They would need the spirits strong and satisfied.

The number of people at the camp began to swell. TV camera crews arrived, but Hutch declined to talk to anyone.

“When it’s over,” he promised.

Angeline could feel the tension growing in the hot air. Then the drum began. The sun continued to climb higher in the sky, and the booming drum seemed to grow more intense with each passing moment. As sweat poured off the foreheads and arms of those drumming and singing, so too, the heat must have assaulted the two men in the railroad car.

“Want to dance?” Angeline asked Jay, almost shouting over the beating drums and song.

“What?” Jay shouted.

“Want to dance?”

“Are you sure?”

“I’m sure.”

The two of them joined the growing circle of dancers raising a cloud of dust around the hot fire and pounding drums. This was the right moment, Angeline thought, and she didn’t even feel silly doing it. She began slowly, just letting the drumbeats tell her what to do. She could feel the drum pounding against her chest.

Her heart, instead of weakening, grew stronger. In time, she danced as if a spirit had taken over, moving her feet and legs. The sensation came back to her, the feeling she’d had the last time she was in this camp, that there were others dancing with her, far more than the number of people in the circle — thousands dancing in rhythm, dancing with one purpose. It was a feeling she'd never experienced before, not even at the best rock concert of her life. They were one living being connected with all living beings: the drummers, the dancers, the plants, the air, the sun above and even the stones, existing for one purpose, and that purpose wasn't copper ore.

XI. The Early Deadline

While others danced, Jay slid onto a stump end next to Hutch and whispered something into his ear. Together, they looked in the direction of the on-the-scene-personality, who waved at them with a nervous look. Hutch stood and walked in her direction, Jay following.

"I was wondering if I could get a statement from you before our early news deadline, something we can use just in case this thing isn't resolved before we go on the air?" she asked.

"I'm a little busy now," Hutch answered.

The on-the-scene-personality was

obviously taken back, a little confused as if no one had rejected their fifteen minutes of fame before, at least not in her presence. Hutch frowned, annoyed as if called out of his grief at a funeral to deal with the caterer. “What do you want?”

“The thing is, the lance. You know. There’s nothing between the train and the mines except the eagle lance. It’s a metaphor, you see? A metaphor for your determination.”

“You’re secularizing it. It’s a prayer to the spirits,” Hutch corrected her.

“That’s it. That’s why you have to explain it. That’s what I love about what you’re doing. You just don’t see people standing up for something because they believe in it. Look at the Persian Gulf War. Who can believe in ‘vital national interests?’ This is different. This is what you believe in,” she argued.

Hutch looked at her closely. She was breathing deeply and her face was flushed. He had seen foreplay that was less effective.

"You're not one of those whites who swears off her own culture and latches onto any minority cause you can find just because it gets your blood moving, are you?" he chastised her. Before she could answer, he jumped back in, feeling his own blood moving. "You have spirits of your own, you know. You have people who hear the spirits speaking to them. But instead of listening, you call them crazy. Did it ever occur to you that Western culture has more words for 'crazy' than the Eskimos have for 'snow'? Then, instead of respecting and honoring your savants, you cure them. I pray that the spirits save me from your cures!"

Hutch turned and walked away. Jay had also noticed the on-the-air-personality's flushed face, and lingered a moment.

"On the other hand, you can cure me any time you want," he deadpanned. The TV personality looked at him and frowned. "And you can quote me on that," Jay said and walked away.

XII. Behind the Scenes

Equilibrium was busy at the miniature golf course on the Island, moving her various people representations around from here to there and there to here, trying to ensure balance with each change. She was so focused on her responsibilities that she didn't see the old man walking up beside her until he was already there. She looked up, saw his warm smile and smiled in return.

"Mind if I join you?" Grandfather asked.

In answer she scooted to the side to make room.

XIII. The Negotiation

The railroad men didn't move and didn't leave the safety of their vehicle. Occasionally, the sound of voices edged with electronic static wafted from that direction, but nothing changed. Time passed.

In the late afternoon, with the sun beating down on them relentlessly, the warriors took a break — a chance to drink water, pour water over long black hair already dripping wet from sweat. Hutch walked over to the railroad car to offer cold water to the railroad men. This time they accepted and drank deeply, removing their caps and wiping sweat from their brows, the edges of their hair wet and matted.

The warriors returned to their drumming as if the deep, rhythmic sound and the eagle feather were all that held back the inspection car and the train somewhere behind it. This time they placed the drum directly on the tracks as if the rails would carry the beat to the place where the train waited, its engines idling, for the tracks to clear. The sun passed its peak but the oppressive heat continued.

XIV. The Other Negotiation

"What's all this?" Grandfather asked Equilibrium patiently, sweeping his hand across the miniature golf course. The tone in his voice was respectful, almost reverential.

"It's the real miniature golf course, the way it's supposed to look," she explained, enthused that someone was interested.

"Impressive," he said, nodding his head in approval. "I like it better this way."

"I do, too, but it can be dangerous stuff, you know. I'm trying hard not to mess it all up," she explained.

"I can see that. What's that stone over there?" He pointed.

"That's the Spirit Stone, the one at the museum."

"I know him well. Do you mind if I borrow him for awhile?"

"For how long?" she wanted to know.

"Forever."

She didn't answer right away, as if slowly coming to understand who he was.

"Oh..."

XV. The Choice

It was mid-afternoon when those in the protest camp felt the earth begin to shudder beneath them. Hutch knew what this was all about. He kneeled and felt the rails. As he stood up, his eyes met Angeline's.

"Old Indian trick," he said, and smiled at her. "Everyone!" He raised his arms to get the protesters' attention. "The train is coming. This doesn't change anything. They're just trying to scare us. We still have to stick together."

In the distance the two engines pulling a long silver train of chemical cars appeared in the distance. It was louder than the inspection car, and spewed more diesel stench into the hot air. Radiant heat waves rose from the engines as the train neared the inspection car, slowed, and then stopped, air brakes hissing and popping. Angeline suddenly felt small, very small. All the protesters stood silently and watched.

Norm was staring at the inspection car as if that would inspire some kind of action. Angeline walked over to Norm and stood beside him. Norm looked back at the drummers and nodded in their direction and the song began again, competing with the droning train engines.

The warriors continued singing, drumming and dancing until their structured rhythm was interrupted by the sound of the inspection car's two-way radio. Moments later the inspection car's engine turned over loudly and started.

"What do you think they'll do?" Angeline asked.

"They have one of two choices – forward or back," Norm answered, biting his lip.

"Then let's help them decide," Brewster said. He walked over to the rails, chose a comfortable spot, and sat down. Angeline joined him. Others followed. Hutch walked over the rails and stood beside the lance, his hand resting about halfway up the shaft.

"What's going on now?" they could hear the static-laced voice over the inspection car's radio. They couldn't hear the reply. Then, slowly, the train began backing away, and continued backing until it was out of sight.

The story in the inspection car was different. The two men inside seemed to be arguing with each other about something. Then the driver stepped out and walked toward the protesters until he stood in front of Hutch.

“Uh ...” he stammered. “I was just wondering, if you had some more of that water?”

Hutch smiled and sent someone for a jug. He handed it to the driver who took a long drink from it.

“Take it with you,” Hutch told him. “You can drop it off the next time you’re in the neighborhood.”

The driver returned to the inspection car, put it in reverse and began backing away until it was no more than a distant spot of reflected light to the Anishinabe Ogichidaa, until it disappeared from view, but continued backing up somewhere in their minds.

XVI. Win, Lose, or Draw?

Hutch watched it recede from his vantage point near the lance. Other warriors gathered around him.

“Did we win?” Jay asked him.

Hutch thought about the experiences of his life. He thought about the first time his parents had that look in their eyes that said they had surrendered to the weight they had carried all of their lives. He thought about the angry mobs he had muscled his way through at the boat landings while trying to exercise his treaty rights. He thought about the few successful instances of resistance against overwhelming force he’d witnessed and the ways in which the forces of the world had fought back. Governments and corporations lived longer than any one person and had longer memories than that. They might be gone today and back again in a hundred years. He thought about the ways the powers-that-be could lose and lose and lose again, until you were out of strength to fight anymore. He thought about how they could destroy the habitat that protected you until you were forced to stand naked against them. Did they win? He wasn't certain either. In his lifetime, the Anishinabe had never won much of anything, so he wasn't sure what it looked like.

He knew all of that and yet at this moment he felt good.

"In every way we know how," he said.

XVII. Lift

Angeline watched the eagle perched nearby throughout the final showdown. It sat unmoving, so she did the same. Only when the inspection car was out of sight did the eagle gather itself and soar upward, joining its mate circling overhead.

As if following the suction of air created by the eagle's wings, the oppressive tension seemed to form together into a small whirlwind, spinning and gathering all the energy in that place, rising upward and away. She closed her eyes while the dust swirled around her.

She knew where it was going: to the spirit world where it would expand many, many times before it returned.

"Whatever you do, don't go back to the Island!"

She looked down and saw the two Little People at her feet.

"Not back to the Island!"

She grabbed Ben's arm and pulled him to his feet.

"We have to get back!"

"What?"

"We have to go, now!"

Chapter Twelve

I. There ...

Tom stood behind his makeshift bar at the Burned Down Cafe, casually wiping the counter with a rag, periodically glancing up at the sky. It was growing dark, purple colored clouds growing in the south and heading straight for the Island.

"What do you think?" his newest waitress asked. Tom wrapped an arm around the waitress's hips and glanced back up to the sky.

"We'll know soon."

Lenny came racing up on his bike, scattering gravel as he came to a sudden, sliding stop. "There's gonna be a big blow. Small craft warning and everything."

Tom reached for a knife beneath the counter and raced to the tent corners, cutting rope.

The temptation was to tie everything down. But that would be like trimming in the mainsail, instead of letting it go slack, when you came about. If he opened the seams on his tent, there would be no resistance for the wind to work against. He forgot where he had first learned that trick, but it was his instinct to do the opposite of conventional wisdom anyway.

II. ... and Back

It was all Ben could do, holding onto the boat's wheel, spray from ten-foot waves washing over the bow into his face. Angeline turned away from the oncoming waves, hanging onto whatever rails and posts seemed sturdy enough that they wouldn't wash away unless the boat went first.

"Where did this come from?" Ben shouted.

"The Spirit World!" Angeline shouted in answer.

"The Spirit World can have it back!"

Then, suddenly it stopped, an eerie calm settling over the lake. They looked around, stunned.

"Oh, shit," Ben muttered, cranking up the engine and racing full speed toward the Island. "This can't be good."

III. Duck and Cover

The Madeline Island Museum curator sat at his desk tapping his pencil against the desk calendar, the one with the picture of the haunted roadhouse in southwestern Wisconsin.

From his desk he could see a glass case in the adjoining display room, a case that held many of the Ojibwe artifacts recovered on Madeline Island during one infrastructure project or another.

The curator turned to the window behind his desk and pulled it open. The air was heavy with moisture. The steady stream of tourists had only added to the building's humid environment.

He stood at the window for a moment, leaning on a cane, taking in some of the fresh air, before sitting back down at his desk. Clouds were moving in. The weather was changing suddenly, as it was known to on the Island. No matter. He was safe here. That was the way of it with museums. They were safe, politically correct and everything.

He gathered together a stack of papers, something to occupy his mind while the wind reached a crescendo outside. Some people lost themselves in mind-numbing sit-coms. Others slipped out of the building to smoke a cigarette. He did paperwork.

But this day, nature's powers-that-be conspired against him. As he released the papers and reached down into a lower desk drawer for chewing gum, a violent gust of wind forced its way through his window, scattering those and many other official forms across the room, creating the kind of documentation blizzard governmental bureaucracies routinely threatened against their enemies. The curator dived under his desk, ducked and covered as recommended in the state safety manual.

IV. Celebrity Perspective

The Rev. Olson was looking out the window of his house at a crowd of tourists gathering at the Indian Cemetery. He had become a complete recluse in recent weeks — the price of celebrity. It was sad, he thought, that the collective American curiosity needed this constant feeding. Worse still, he thought, how each of these tourists could ride the ferry to the Island, take their buses to the cemetery, shoot their snapshots posing in front of the cemetery, and never understand any of it. He curbed his judgmental attitude. After all, he had been just like these people once —uninitiated, unknowing. He had learned the hard way, but at least he had learned. He glanced up at the sky. It looked like rain. He would almost enjoy seeing a washout scatter the crowd —

He was interrupted in his revelations by a knocking on the front door.

"Who ...?"

He walked down the long hallway toward the door, pulling it open without thinking. An older man and woman, ebullient in demeanor, holding a disposable camera, stood in his open doorway smiling.

"Excuse me," the woman said, renewing the smile before continuing. "I wonder if we could get a picture of you."

"Oh!" the man interrupted, "with your croquet mallet if it's handy."

The Rev. Olson's jaws tightened, but he said nothing, simply closing the door on the couple, then walking back to the window where at least he could feel superior in peace.

The wind was beginning to blow, scattering small twigs, then hats, and then tourists. Only after the tourists rushed to the safety of their bus, did he notice the small, fragile looking woman near the cemetery entrance. She looked familiar, very familiar. He might never forget that tank top T-shirt. That's when the wind accelerated, throwing clouds of dust against the young woman, then felling large branches from trees, even knocking sailboats from their cradles in the marina storage yard.

The Rev. Olson didn't have to think, only react. He ran for the front door, flinging it open and leaving it open behind him, running out into the storm and toward the figure now huddled on the ground.

V. Hole-in-One

Tom retreated back behind the bar as the wind rolled across the Island, carrying dust and debris in its advance wave. He smiled smugly to himself as canvas and ropes flapped in the breeze. It was one thing to be a burned down cafe, but another thing altogether to be a blown-away cafe. As a practical matter, his clients expected his business to open the doors, if it had doors, at the same location every night. It wouldn't do to move just now, even if only to a neighboring Island.

"Looks like we carry on," he said to his newest bartender, wrapping an arm around her as if anchoring her against the wind.

He wasn't as fortunate with his prize sculpture, his prehistoric Ford pickup. When the wind caught it at the stern, it didn't take much force to get it moving. Tom spotted the motion before the sculpture left his yard. He looked along the line of its probable path and decided that, if he hesitated another ten seconds, there would be no reversing fate.

"Aren't you going to stop it?" his bartender who wasn't an archeologist asked.

The dinosaur rolled down the alley until it glanced off a pile of debris, heading straight for the miniature golf course.

" ... three, two, one. Oops. Too late," he deadpanned. "Hole-in-one …"

VI. Balance Restored

Covering her head was just a precaution. The truth was, Equilibrium found the wind exciting and the rain refreshing. She suspected something important was happening, in a cosmic kind of way. She knew it for certain when she saw the fat man leaning over her shouting, "Are you OK? Are you OK?"

Then the wind and rain stopped, completely. She knew just what to do.

"Hurry!" she urged him, racing toward the cemetery, pulling him with her. "Hurry, before the balance shifts again!"

They raced through the wildflowers and weeds to Madeline's tilted headstone.

"Give me all your coins! Hurry!"

He did as he was told, reaching into his pocket and pulling out a handful, pouring them into her hands. She carefully arranged them in stacks on top of the tombstone, then sighed, kneeling down beside the grave.

"Just in time." She looked back over her shoulder at the Rev. Olson. "The balance is back."

VII. The Escape

The dust was settling as Ben's boat coasted into the marina. Angeline and Ben stared at the damage, debris strewn everywhere, boats lying on their sides, a few trees down, and outhouses toppled. Bens glorified tugboat glided to the main dock where Angeline jumped, rope in hand, to tie the boat up.

The two of them walked along the main street, their heads turning in every direction.

People slowly emerged from the various places they had sought shelter. She noted that the crowd exiting the men's restroom at the Town Dock were not all men. That said something for their sanity, that they didn't think twice about abandoning decorum when it seemed like the world was coming to an end.

There was a police car at the main intersection with its red lights flashing, a patrolman in a yellow rain slicker directing traffic around a horizontal spruce. The landscape looked foreign, almost alien. It must have seemed that way to everyone who had shared the experience. The faces of those milling about looked confused. People in the crowd walked slowly, if at all, glancing all about as if not sure what parts of the earth, lake, and sky they could trust.

Angeline had seen this before. It was part of her imprinting. She understood the cumulative forces that had built to this explosive climax. They had to happen.

They couldn't help it.

She wandered past the ferry and then the miniature golf course, amused that a prehistoric Ford was now parked there.

As if on some cue Angeline missed, everyone around her fell to the ground. Then, two harmonic voices diverted her attention.

"Don't look there!"

"Not there!"

Of course, she looked and saw him, the little, wiry, brown man walking through the crowd and around the debris, heading with deliberate steps toward the ferry dock, a heavy stone perched on his shoulder.

He was a strange sight, surrounded by strange sights. Maybe that's why no one else seemed to notice, but to her it was as obvious as a bear living under a porch. He seemed too frail to carry his own bones, let alone a heavy stone that must have weighed more than a hundred pounds. She turned to someone standing next to her, a stranger with a shared trauma, whose eyes seemed fixed on nothing at all. She was going to point out the little man, maybe to verify what she saw, but knew it would be useless, a wasted effort. When she looked back to the little man, walking away from her now, he turned his head back to her, smiled and winked, as if acknowledging this little secret that they shared.

She felt a hand on her shoulder.

"Did you see that?" It was Ben.

"See what?" she asked.

"That lightning. That was close."

She couldn't imagine how she missed it, unless she'd been standing too close.

Epilogue

I. The Guardian

From the time of the Ghost Dance in the 1890s, until 1978 it was illegal for Native American tribes to practice their religious beliefs in Wissconsin.

There had been other, less obvious, problems to deal with, too.

Whites who openly professed their bigotry could make those same religious practices dangerous. No Ku Klux Klan was needed. The cavalry had performed the moral majority's dirty work in those days.

But equally hazardous were the whites who claimed to hold the Native Americans' best interests at heart. They encouraged the tribes to join Christian churches, worship the white man's angry god, wear white clothes, go to mission schools, learn English and forget their native languages.

The wars between the Indians and the U.S. Army were not solely a demonstration of the white race's superior armaments.

They were also intended as a demonstration of cultural superiority. How could the tribes hope to compete against the culture which gave the world gunpowder-propelled metal projectiles and, subsequently, gasoline-propelled piston engines, Freon-propelled refrigeration, radio wavelength-propelled television, hydrogen-propelled nuclear weapons and microwave-propelled ovens.

Clearly, in the eyes of Western civilization, the Native American culture, which had produced nothing more clever than harmony with nature, was inferior.

In that case, it was incumbent on the Native Americans to accept their fate and be assimilated, went the prevailing thought. It was as inevitable as taxes.

The trail led back as far as the early nineteenth century when documents outlined a U.S. government policy designed to encourage tribal debts that, in turn, would be forgiven as the tribes surrendered more and more land to settle those debts. It was such a capitalistic means of overwhelming detractors. First, impose the economic system on your enemies, then run up the debt load. Kill them softly with a high credit line.

In time, the number of Indians would decrease until, according to policy advisors of the time, none would remain.

Angeline owned no gun-powder propelled metal projectiles, or anything powered by hydrogen, Freon, or microwaves. Her Suzuki used gas, but it was questionable just how much longer. She heated her coffee in a tin pot on the campfire. She had no debt load.

Instead, she listened during the night for sounds and read meaning into them. She calibrated her life to the changing weather every day. She talked with spirits regularly, almost as often as she conversed with tourists, and preferred her conversations with spirits.

This night she heard his footsteps behind her as he approached the fire.

"The coffee's almost ready."

"Good. I've had a busy day. I could

use a cup," he said wearily, sitting on a stump end across from her. He pulled his hand-woven Indian blanket close around his shoulders and she did the same with her Norwegian quilt.

"I'm surprised you can still walk. That was a heavy load you were carrying."

"He's not so heavy when he wants to move, and he was ready, now that there's Anishinabe on the Island again."

"Who?"

"You, of course. He couldn't leave until there was somebody here to watch over things."

She shivered. Suddenly she felt a weight on her shoulders.

"I don't know if I can – "

"I thought, many years ago, that you were just the one. I was certain today when you learned to see the world the way it really is, to see in the Spirit World."

"Learned what?"

"Everyone in the physical world saw a flash of lightning. You saw me and the Spirit Stone. Here, come with me. There's something I want to show you." He stood stiffly, lifted a burning tree branch from the fire, and began walking through the woods, the flame lighting the way. She stepped in his exact footsteps, ducking under overhanging tree branches, over fallen logs and around mounds of earth. Finally, he stopped, holding the torch out over a tree stump elevated by a particularly large earthen mound.

"What do you see?"

She looked. "A tree stump and a mound of dirt," she answered.

"No, look again. Look with your heart, not your head."

She did as he instructed, closing her eyes, aware of her heartbeat now strong and vibrant. When she opened her eyes, this time she could see it, and others like it surrounding her camp, burial sites she had never even been aware of before.

“There are many of them on the Island, your ancestors and my descendants. This one in particular was cleverly hidden for hundreds of years. I thought the tree was a nice touch. No one would mess with it when there was a tree growing from it. Then a few years ago, in a storm like today, the tree went down, and that was that. This one needs protection now, and that one and that one and that one,” he said, pointing with his lips in many directions. "I thought many years ago that you were just the one. I was certain today when, instead of a flash of lightning, you saw me, and now, I know you see what others can’t. All I ask is that you do your best to take care of us.” This time when he looked up at her, the flame from the burning branch illuminating his face, she saw a tear rolling down his cheek.

“Of course, but how?”

He smiled. “You know how. You can’t help yourself.”

She smiled in return.

“Come back to the fire with me. Have some coffee. We’ll talk before you go."

"No," he answered handing her the burning branch. "This is where I stay, for awhile anyway." He sat down on the tree stump. "I'm tired. I need some rest. You go. It's a beautiful night. Enjoy it."

She turned to go. After a couple of steps, he called to her.

"Hey!" She turned back. "You might need this." He removed his Indian blanket and tossed it to her. She caught it with her free hand and draped it over one shoulder. "It gets cold in the winter."

"Goodbye," she said.

"You know where to find me if you need me."

She turned away and went back to her campfire. She poured herself a cup of coffee, and then filled a second one, a spirit cup, just in case.

II. Dreams

Angeline fought off sleep that night as long as she could, but despite strong coffee, the rhythmic wave action lulled her into that place between wakefulness and sleep. She continued to fight it, the way she'd fought her adopted mother when it was time to dress up in pink dresses with her hair tied in a red ribbon for what seemed like an eternal drive to church. She resisted passively, yet aggressively, the way she'd braced her legs against learning the catechism and the myriad guilts she really had no talent for. She rebelled, the way she'd run to a series of jobs waitressing, pizza-delivering, and nursing-home-care-taking just to get out of the house. Finally, she tried to assert her truth over it all, the way she'd taken control in the final days of her adoptive father's life, nursing him, washing him, medicating him, listening to the simple truths of his life, all the while arranging the funeral and burial.

None of it worked. Dreams overcame her.

They arrived like a flood she knew was there but could never openly acknowledge, not even to herself, as if she still heard her mother's pinch-mouthed warning: "We will never speak of this again."

In her dreams, she felt her mother, her real mother, as a steady heartbeat, with a glimpse of golden hair, and a loving, if sad, presence.

She dreamed of confronting her adoptive mother after the funeral, listening to her cynical confession: Yes, she'd tried to raise her daughter the right way, in the church, with all the advantages, holding in her frustrations and disappointments trying everything she knew, except just loving her. And hearing her adoptive mother say, "Well, I guess we were just awful parents if we did so many things wrong," her lips compressed into the same thin line they always formed when she was being defensive, and Angeline feeling, for the first time, pity for the woman who could take nothing from motherhood but feelings of inadequacy. It wasn't the same as love, this pity, but it was a feeling anyway.

And she dreamed of the time when she almost got married, when they realized, after the flush of their decision, that it was wrong. The realization was mutual and simultaneous. They looked at each other, looked away quickly, and just knew.

And finally she dreamed of walking along the beach with her bear, her hand resting on his shoulders, her fingers only slightly enmeshed with his fur, as they casually left their footprints in the sand, Angeline walking on the water side, feeling the soothing coolness from incoming waves on her feet.

These weren't signature dreams, they were not life-defining symbolic codes. This was not Black Elk seeing the renewal of the world and telling it to his people. This was not a vision quest. There was no single message she could take from any one of them, but collectively they said, "You can dream now, because you dream so well and because dreaming is good."

III. Woman Who Returns

She awoke early, early enough to see the sunrise while the smell of freshly brewed coffee warmed the air around her campfire, before the wildflowers reopened their petals to the sun, and long before whatever era would inevitably follow the computer age.

She felt a little smug. The sunrise had been spectacular. She'd seen a part of the day few people appreciated, not the sailboat captains still tightly coiled with a tourist or two in the V-berths of luxury sailboats; not Tom, who never saw the sunrise unless he stayed up that late; she was up earlier than Ben, whose day didn't start until he walked into hell and downed a half-pot of coffee. It seemed early enough to make her feel young again.

She warmed herself wrapped in her new blanket until the sun rose high enough to finish the job. She delayed going back to The Restaurant, knowing work would be a letdown, knowing she wasn't quite ready to deal with life's insistent minutiae. The Island people would be cleaning up the debris today, but they could do it without her.

Once she felt like a warm-blooded

animal again, she thought it might be a good day to start her new job, the job of protecting the Island.

She drove her Suzuki to the north shore, then followed the familiar path to the burial grounds, walked around to make certain that all was well, left some tobacco and started walking back to her car. She met Orchid on the way.

“I can’t stay long," Orchid acknowledged. “My mother’s waiting in the car and, you know ...”

She knew.

A flock of seagulls circled, then landed in the water below the two women, bobbing up and down on the playful waves.

“I have a gift for you,” Orchid announced. “I had a dream about your ancestors. All your ancestors going back to the beginning of time were there. They told me to give you your Indian name. Your name is now Azhegiiwequay,” she told her, then repeated it so Angeline could practice it for awhile.

"What does it mean?" Angeline asked.

"Woman Who Returns," Orchid told her. "We'll have to have a naming ceremony and a feast, but I wanted you to know as soon as possible."

In exchange for the gift, Angeline gave Orchid the ring she'd received from the little old lady in the nursing home in Minneapolis, the one who could swear like a truck driver. The two women's personalities couldn't be more different, but both had perfected their lives. Orchid thanked her and stood up. She had to go. Her mother ...

Angeline then walked to the ferry dock and a familiar phone booth there. She arranged all her change in neat stacks and dialed the number.

"Hello?"

"Hi."

"Who is this?"

Angeline let her annoyance fly away on the morning's gentle breeze.

“It’s me, Angeline.”

“It’s about time you called.”

“I know. I’m sorry about that. I’ll try to call more often from now on.”

IV. One Last Thing

There was one more task Angeline had left, something she’d been saving for just the right time. She drove her Suzuki through dissipating mists to the ferry, rode the first ferry of the day to the mainland, drove along the coast a few miles, and parked in front of a familiar historic marker.

There, she put her artistic training to work. Matching the highway department’s brown and cream colors was more challenging than she’d anticipated but, once finished, the distant Island emerging under the morning sun had been renamed. It was now, “Equaysayway Island.” She couldn’t help herself.

She knew it wouldn’t last. The first time a road crew passed it ... well, it might take longer than that. State employees were notorious for neglecting problems that created more work. Then, there would be the usual bureaucratic tussle over who had jurisdiction. Sooner or later someone with enough political clout would demand that history be set right. In the meantime, a few tourists would be misinformed and some of those might go a lifetime without being "set right."

The odds were good, and then who could predict the repercussions?